Soft Shoulder

by

Robert Baty

The Wild Rose Press, Inc.
PO Box 708
Adams Basin, NY 14410-0708
Visit us at www.thewildrosepress.com

Publishing History
First Edition, 2024
Trade Paperback ISBN 978-1-5092-5739-3
Digital ISBN 978-1-5092-5740-9

Published in the United States of America

Dedication

For Gail

Chapter 1

Soon as I called, she cut to the chase and told me cellphones sucked in the hills. If I wanted to talk about Archie, I could come up to the house for lemonade. Say around two? The *she* was Daphne Swan, widow of the late Archie Gibbs. I did want to talk about Archie, but only because he was dead. My name's McQuinn, but most people call me Max. I'm a reporter assigned to obituaries at the *Bay Area Bugle*, and I was on deadline for Archie's obit.

Most of the people I covered were famous in one way or another. If they made news when they were alive, they would make news when they passed away. Gangsters, celebrities, politicians, sports heroes, astronauts, pop stars—hell, even thieves like Archie Gibbs. I covered them all as they shuffled past my desk on their way to the grave.

All I knew about Gibbs was what everybody else knew, and that was enough for 800 words in the morning edition. He was a master thief who'd robbed banks, hijacked armored cars, held up big rigs at gunpoint, and even boosted containers filled with Korean electronics from the Port of Oakland. Archie didn't always get away with it and spent as much time behind bars as he did outside prison walls. But doing time never stopped him. In fact, Archie saw it as the cost of doing business.

Daphne was Archie's third wife, half his age and

married for just a couple of years. But she was present at the end, which made her a good place to start. If she was offering lemonade, maybe she'd bring out some cookies too. I didn't much care for lemonade, but if it came with some inside dope on where Archie stashed the loot from his last big score, I might stick around for a refill.

Twenty minutes after paying the Richmond Bridge toll and crossing San Pablo Bay, I took the Lucas Valley exit off 101 North and drove into the hills. The views got better the higher I went, and I figured so did the rents. When I reached the crest, I could see the Golden Gate Bridge and the San Francisco skyline.

As I drove through the blind curves that fishtailed into the hills, I passed a house that was under construction. Nobody seemed to be working on the house, and I wondered if the workers had taken the day off. But then, out of the corner of my eye, I thought I saw someone sunbathing on the deck. I tossed the car through a few more curves, then pulled up in front of a rambling ranch style house with a king-size lawn and a two-car garage.

There was a "For Sale" sign planted in the grass and a convertible waiting in the driveway, top down, leather seats getting hot in the sun. I figured now that Archie had moved on, Daphne was planning to do likewise. I parked next to the convertible, then got out of the car and went up to the house and rang the bell.

But nobody came to the door. I waited until I got tired of waiting, then rang the bell again. This time I heard a woman I figured was Daphne yell, "Coming!"

Then the door opened.

"Hi, sorry to keep you waiting," she said. "I took a dip in the pool and forgot what time it was." She stuck out her hand. "I'm Daphne Swan."

Her name rolled off her lips like a line of poetry.

"Max McQuinn, *Bay Area Bugle*," I said, but it didn't have quite the same ring to it.

She was barefoot and wearing a terrycloth robe, and her auburn hair was dripping wet. She was in her thirties, more or less, with big dark eyes and high cheekbones. She had the kind of face you saw on magazine covers. I wondered if that was where Archie found her. And yet, there was a kind of disappointment in her face, as if her beauty hadn't taken her as far as it should have.

"Come in," she said, "we can talk out by the pool."

I followed her into the house, and she closed the door behind me. It was cool and dark in the living room, and for a minute I wondered if Archie was hiding in the shadows. But the way she walked across the room toward the sliding glass doors that led to the pool made me forget all about him.

We went outside and sat at a patio table near the deep end. I noticed that there was a pitcher of lemonade and two glasses on the table. She may have forgotten about the time, but apparently not about the lemonade.

"Beautiful day, isn't it?" she said, shading her eyes as she looked up at the sky.

I figured it was always a beautiful day if you were Daphne Swan. I looked up at the sky and smiled, and left it at that.

Daphne poured two glasses and handed one to me.

"So refreshing on a hot day, don't you think?" she said.

For a minute it was easy to forget that I was there to talk about her dead husband. Maybe that was because Daphne didn't seem broken up about it. But I'd been in

3

obits long enough to know that people grieved in different ways, and maybe sitting in the sun with a glass of lemonade was the way Daphne Swan got through it all. Who was I to know? I was just the guy who wrote the obituary. That didn't mean I knew a damn thing about what went on in people's hearts.

Daphne sipped her lemonade, then set the glass down on the table and looked at me. "So I guess we better talk about Archie. That's why you're here, right?"

I nodded because it was the truth. But it was also true that I would have been happy to talk about anything else. Death didn't become her, maybe because she was anything but dead. In my experience, grief had a way of making the survivors seem as if they too were somehow dead. Daphne wasn't like that. She may have been grieving, but it wasn't killing her.

"What would you like to know about my husband?"

"Well, first, I'd like to say thanks for meeting with me. I know from experience that this isn't an easy time."

Daphne gave a sad smile. She lowered her eyes. "Never had anybody die on me before…and then it turns out to be Archie."

I took out my voice recorder and set it on the table. "Mind if I record our conversation?"

Daphne shook her head. "Sure, no problem."

I switched on the recorder and looked at her. "What do you think would be the best word to describe your husband?"

Daphne seemed to stiffen at the question. "You mean besides crook?"

She took me by surprise. I offered an awkward smile. "I didn't mean it that way," I said.

"But he was a crook, right?"

I paused. Archie was a crook, no doubt about it, and he left behind the rap sheet to prove it. But I wasn't here to speak ill of the dead.

"I'm sure that's not all he was," I said.

"No, it wasn't. He was the sweetest guy in the world, really. Not that you'd know it if all you knew about him was what you saw on the six o' clock news."

"How'd you meet him?"

"Vegas, where else?"

I smiled.

"But I wasn't a showgirl, okay?" Daphne said, wanting to set the record straight. "I wasn't taking my clothes off or anything like that."

"What were you doing?"

"I was a dealer at one of the casinos."

"Which one?"

"I worked at a bunch of 'em while I was there, but the night I met Archie I was working at The Flamingo."

"So what happened?"

Daphne shrugged. "I don't know, exactly. I guess he just played his cards right."

"You weren't together long, right?"

A shadow fell across Daphne's face and stayed there. "Not long enough, that's for sure."

Daphne fell silent. A breeze drifted across the pool, stirring the water. How long is long enough, I wondered. I'd interviewed surviving spouses who'd been married for decades, and not one of them ever told me they'd been together long enough.

"So how come you haven't asked me the big question?" Daphne said, interrupting my thoughts.

I looked up at her and smiled. "You don't waste time, do you, Daphne?"

She looked off in the distance at nothing in particular.

"What's the point? It's all anybody wants to know."

Suddenly, the doorbell rang. I was surprised we could hear it out by the pool, but I figured it was because Daphne had left the sliding doors open. She tensed at the sound and looked toward the house. The doorbell rang again, but Daphne didn't move to answer it.

"You want to get that?" I said, switching off the recorder.

She glanced at me, and the look in her eyes told me it was the last thing she wanted to do.

Whoever was ringing the bell decided to do it the old-fashioned way, and started pounding on the door. Daphne jumped out of her chair. Her arm flew across the table and knocked over her glass. But she barely seemed to notice the lemonade washing across the table.

Because the next thing we heard was the sound of the door crashing open and heavy footsteps coming toward us. Then a pair of mooks who looked as if they'd stumbled out of stir appeared at the sliding glass doors.

One of them was muscle-bound and bald, with a slab for a face. He looked to be in his fifties, and he wore a denim shirt with the sleeves rolled up to show off the crude prison tattoos that defaced his forearms. His buddy was a dumb-eyed kid with a skinny build, a bony face and greasy, slicked-back hair. He wore a faded black T-shirt with the name of some rock band I never heard of, jeans, and hiking boots.

I stood at the sight of them, then glanced at Daphne. She was gripping the back of the chair with both hands and I noticed that her knuckles had turned white.

"Who are these guys, Daphne?" I said, suddenly

afraid for her.

But she was too busy staring at her visitors to answer me. I could see the fear in her eyes as they scowled at her.

"You didn't come to the door so we decided to let ourselves in," Bodybuilder said.

Rocker giggled. "Sorry about the door."

"What do you want?"

"You know what we want."

"I told you the last time you barged in on me. I don't know anything about it."

"Yeah, that's what you said."

"Trouble is, it still ain't the truth," Bodybuilder said. Then it was my turn. "Who the fuck are you?"

"I'm a reporter."

"Yeah? What the fuck you doin' here?"

"I'm writing Archie's obituary."

"No shit?" Rocker looked at his buddy. "So maybe she told him?"

"Yeah, maybe."

They stepped out into the patio and came up to the table. Daphne tried to back away, but there was nowhere to go except into the deep end. Bodybuilder glared at Daphne, then turned to me.

"She tell you about it?"

"Tell me about what?"

Bodybuilder's face hardened. He took a step closer to me, then reached behind his back and pulled a gun. A 9mm semiautomatic from the looks of it.

"Don't play fuckin' dumb with me!" he said, the gun in my face at point-blank range.

I froze. Stared down the barrel like it was a tunnel to my immediate future. I wrote obituaries for a living, but at the moment I wondered if I was about to become the subject of an obit, rather than its author.

"What are you gonna do, Roy? Shoot us?" Daphne said.

Out of the corner I could see she was trembling and trying hard not to show it.

"Yeah, maybe I will, just for fun."

Rocker's face fell. "We can't shoot 'em, Roy…they ain't told us nothin' yet."

I wondered if the guy had just figured out the dead don't talk.

"Put the gun down, Roy," Daphne said in a calm tone of voice, as if it wasn't the first time she'd seen him reach for it. "He doesn't know anything either. He's just writing Archie's obituary, okay?"

Roy swung the gun to Daphne.

"But you know all about it, don't you, Daphne?"

Daphne sighed. "How many times do I have to tell you I don't know?"

"As many times as it takes until you do know."

"You know what, Roy? Why don't you shove the gun up your ass and get the hell off my property."

Roy flew into a rage. "I want my share!" he yelled loud enough for the neighbors to hear if there were any neighbors.

Then, as if that wasn't enough, he jabbed Daphne in the ribs with the gun, causing her to lose her balance. She let go of the chair and tipped backward toward the pool. I reached out and grabbed her before she fell into the water.

"You want your share, Roy?" she said, breathless, her eyes filling with tears.

"Yeah, I want my share!" He jabbed a fat thumb at

his chest. "I got it comin'!"

Daphne smiled bitterly and locked eyes with Roy.

"Go ask Archie where he hid it."

That seemed to take the wind out of him. The gun hung at his side, as if he didn't know what else to do with it. But I figured that sooner or later it was going to go off.

Daphne pointed toward the sliding glass doors. "The door's over there, in case you forgot," she said.

Roy scowled at her, then shoved the gun in his waistband. He nodded at Rocker, and they turned and walked away. I could hear their footsteps on the hardwood floor in the living room, but I didn't hear the front door slam, probably because they'd broken the lock.

"Sorry about that," Daphne said. She slumped in a chair, her face creased with worry.

Lemonade was dripping off the table, but Daphne barely seemed to notice it.

"You okay?" I said.

Daphne nodded. "Yeah, I'm okay," she said, in a weary tone of voice that suggested she was anything but okay.

"Who were those guys?"

"Roy and Donny. They were in Archie's gang, did a couple of jobs with him."

"Including the last one, right?" I said. "The Paycheck Today job."

Daphne looked at me, surprised. "You know about that?"

"I heard the rumors, about how nobody knows what happened to the goods."

"Archie knows, and he's not talking," Daphne said.

"So he never told you about it?"

Daphne shook her head. "Hard to believe, right? I think he was worried that if he told me about it, I'd take the money and run." She gave a sad smile. "I thought he knew me better than that." She fell silent for a moment, as if to allow herself a memory of Archie. "The funny part is that I could really use it now that he's gone."

"What about his will? He must have left you with something."

Daphne scoffed. "Yeah, a mortgage I can't afford. Archie didn't think much about the future. He spent all he had in the present."

"I saw the 'For Sale' sign out front."

Daphne nodded. "I can't afford the house now that he's gone."

"Where you gonna go?"

Daphne shrugged. "Someplace where those goons can't find me."

I stuck around until Daphne found a locksmith to come up and fix the front door, then I headed back to the office. I was still on deadline, but I wasn't thinking about Archie Gibbs anymore. I was thinking about the gun in my face and hoping it wasn't pointed at me when it went off.

Chapter 2

I ran into Nicole as I stepped off the elevator on the third floor of the *Bugle* building on Mission Street in downtown San Francisco.

"Hey you," she said. "How it go with the widow Gibbs?"

"Fine," I said, "except for the part with the gun."

Nic's eyes widened. She covered crime for the paper, and guns always got her attention. I often wondered if the fact that her father had been an Army sniper had something to do with it.

"What gun?"

"I'll tell you later, after I'm done."

"You better," Nic said.

I smiled. "I promise. You'll love it."

I settled into my cubicle and fired up my computer. Then I went over my notes to see if I'd missed anything. But I hadn't. I remembered every detail, starting with Daphne in her bathrobe and ending with a gun in my face. I wasn't the only one who wanted to know what happened to the Paycheck Today heist. But if Archie took the secret with him to his grave, then he may as well have taken the loot with him too.

I knocked out a draft that left out the part about the goons and the gun and sent it to Jack the Ripper, aka my editor. I figured Daphne didn't need the tabloid attention that would bring, or maybe I was just trying to protect

11

her. But that wasn't my job. I was a reporter. My job was to report what happened, not leave out what happened. My first mistake. While I was waiting for the Ripper's review, my thoughts circled back to the woman who offered me lemonade. I wondered what else she had to offer. Trouble, I figured, with plenty of refills.

A shadow fell across my cubicle. I looked up and saw the Ripper taking up space, a hardcopy of Archie's obit in his hand.

"Where's the bloody juice, mate?"

The Ripper was a skinny Brit in his fifties, with red hair, a fat mustache, and freckles. His real name was Dickie Swift, but Nicole and I called him the Ripper because he had an annoying habit of ripping up copy and headlines he didn't like and dumping the shredded remains on your desk. Dickie had worked on the Fleet Street tabloids before he fled to the States, and I figured that was why he always wanted the dirt, as if obits were like the tabloids. Especially when the subject was a bigshot like Archie Briggs.

"She didn't have much to say. I figured she was still in shock."

"Nothing on the Paycheck Today job then?"

I shook my head. "I don't think she knows anything about it."

The Ripper frowned. He glanced at the hardcopy in his hand. "Underworld Kingpin Dead at 68, Takes Secret with Him to His Grave," he said, reading the headline aloud.

"Okay with you?" I said.

Dickie shrugged. "It's all we got, right?"

I nodded.

"Run it."

He shoved the hardcopy into my hand and walked back to his office.

****

Nic bought the first round. We were down the street at Dewey's, an afterwork dive sandwiched between a nail salon and a Chinese restaurant that made pretty good potstickers.

"You think she knows?" she said after I filled her in on the afternoon's events at Daphne's house.

I shrugged. "If she does so she's not letting on. But I'm sure she'd like to get her hands on it, just like the goons who showed up at the house. But Archie left 'em all hanging."

"I wonder why."

"Maybe just to get the last laugh."

"What do you mean?"

"Maybe it wasn't about the money for him. Maybe it was about pulling off the biggest heist of his life and then burying the treasure somewhere so nobody could ever find it."

"Doesn't make sense. Why would he go through all the trouble?"

"Just to prove he could do it and get away with it."

"Now everybody's chasing the loot, right?"

I nodded. "And Archie's somewhere laughing his ass off."

Nic frowned. "The dead don't laugh, Max."

I shrugged. "Just a thought."

"Did you think the guy was gonna shoot you?"

I knocked back the rest of my drink. "It occurred to me. Doesn't take much to squeeze a trigger. Especially when you're pissed."

"Can't believe this happened to you. You've got the

safest job in the world. I mean, how much trouble can dead people cause?"

"I think I'm starting to find out," I said.

"I thought trouble was my beat, Max."

I gave a rueful smile. "So did I."

I glanced at Nicole. She was in her thirties and looked like an athlete. She had short blonde hair, blue eyes, and the kind of clear complexion that came from not having impure thoughts. But I wasn't sure about that last part. What I was sure of was that she my best friend at the paper.

"Did you tell the Ripper what happened?" she said.

I shook my head.

"Why not?"

"You know Dickie. He's always looking for the dirt. If I told him what happened there'd be a bunch of reporters barging in on her wanting all the juicy details."

"You're not falling for her, are you, Max?"

I looked up at her. She was giving me that knowing smile of hers, the one that always annoyed me because it usually meant she was right.

"So what'd I miss while I was out having fun?" I said, changing the subject.

Nic shrugged. "You name it. Burglary, larceny, armed robbery, breaking and entering, auto theft, smash and grab, aggravated assault. You want to hear my favorite?"

"I do, but I think we need another round."

Nic grinned as I flagged a bartender and pointed at our glasses.

"You ready?" she said.

"Ready."

"A couple out in the Avenues discovered a burglar

in their house when the husband told his wife a joke and they heard somebody laugh upstairs."

I stared at Nicole as a smile spread across my face.

"You're kidding me."

Nicole shook her head.

"That really happened?"

"Pretty funny, huh?"

"Hilarious."

We called it a night after that. I was on deadline with the recently departed but still famous, and Nicole had called a meeting with a CI named Rikers who was only available after hours. She shared him with a homicide cop she'd dated who worked for the SFPD. The way the story went, Rikers' mother was pregnant when she visited her husband on Rikers Island. She went into labor while she was there and gave birth in the prison infirmary. Just seemed like a no-brainer to call the kid Rikers. His tips enabled Nicole to break stories ahead of just about every other crime reporter in town. Nobody knew exactly how she did it and Nic wasn't talking.

I used to think that our beats were separated by the gulf between life and death, but after what happened at Daphne's house, I wasn't so sure anymore.

Then, a little after midnight, the phone rang.

****

The lights were on when I got to the house. The convertible was in the driveway and the top was still down. Only now instead of getting hot in the sun the seats were slick with mist. I knew I shouldn't be there. I knew if I was smart I'd turn around and drive back home and pretend like her phone call never happened. Instead, I parked next to the convertible and killed the lights.

Then two shots rang out.

Flashes of gunfire lit up the windows.

I stopped cold, half out of the car. Before I could decide what to do next, the front door flew open and Donny came out of the house. He was still wearing the same T-shirt, only now the band's logo was drenched with blood. He staggered across the lawn until he got as far as the "For Sale" sign, then collapsed face down in the grass.

I jumped out of the car and ran into the house. Daphne was standing in the living room wearing a pair of silk pajamas. I wondered if she ever got dressed. There was a gun in her hand. When I saw Roy bleeding out on the carpet I knew why.

I stared at his corpse as if I was in a dream. As if I'd never left the house and was still safely asleep. But I wasn't asleep, and I sure as hell wasn't safe. The acrid smell of cordite clung to the air.

"I had to do it," Daphne said. "They were gonna kill me."

"Both of 'em?" I said, unable to take my eyes off the body on the carpet.

"They broke in, I was asleep, I heard them in the house," she said in a breathless voice. "They said they just wanted to talk but I knew they wanted to kill me…"

It didn't make sense, I thought. Even a mook as dumb as Donny had figured out that there was no percentage in killing somebody before they told you what you wanted to know.

"It was self-defense, you have to believe me."

I shook my head. "The cops have to believe you, Daphne, not me. You called 'em, right?"

"The cops? Are you kidding? I was Archie's wife, okay? A gangster's wife. They think I know all about the heist and where he hid the loot. They're just waiting for me to make a move before they arrest me. They've been here twice already asking questions since Archie died. What do you think they're gonna do when I tell 'em it was them or me?"

"It's the truth, isn't it, Daphne?"

I didn't have a clue whether it was the truth or not, but I figured I'd give her a chance to convince me. Maybe if I believed her the cops would too.

"Of course it's the truth. You think I murdered them in cold blood? Is that what you think?"

"They're dead, aren't they?"

"There's a difference between murder and self-defense."

"Yeah, there is. Maybe you should call your lawyer and let him explain it to you."

She came up to me and took my hand like we knew each other better than we did.

"I don't need a lawyer, Max. I just need you."

I felt the ground shift beneath my feet. Things were spinning seriously out of control. What did she want me to do? Bury the bodies in the backyard, clean the carpets, wipe away the fingerprints, spray a little air freshener to get rid of the smell? And then what—live happily ever after?

"Why'd you call me?"

"I got scared. I didn't want to be alone. I didn't know who else to call."

"And now that I'm here I guess you want me help you clean up a crime scene, right?"

"Don't say it like that."

"How should I say it, Daphne? You got a body on the floor and another guy on the lawn with his arm wrapped around the 'For Sale' sign. What happens when it gets light out? You gonna leave him there? Your real estate agent's not gonna like that."

Daphne's eyes widened. Her hand flew to her mouth. "Oh my God!"

"What is it?"

"I totally forgot—my agent scheduled an open house on Sunday."

I tried not to laugh. "You're kidding me. An open house? I think you better cancel."

Daphne shook her head. "I can't cancel."

"Why not?"

"I can't. If I don't sell now the bank is gonna foreclose on the house."

"Speaking of houses, I saw a place down the road," I said. "Looked like it was under construction. Any chance somebody could have heard the shots?"

Daphne shook her head. "A contractor was building it on spec. He ran out of money and it's been abandoned ever since."

"You sure? I thought I saw somebody up there when I drove by this afternoon."

"There's nobody home," Daphne said. "Nothing we have to worry about."

Nothing we have to worry about, the lady said. Like we were in this together and there was no way out. But there was a way out. It was called the front door. All I needed to do was walk through it and get back in the car and try not to look at the guy on the lawn as I backed out of the driveway.

"You want a drink?" Daphne said, interrupting my thoughts.

I looked at her. "What, is it happy hour?"

"I just thought you might need a drink."

She was right. I did need a drink. But that wasn't going to fix anything. She walked over to a liquor cabinet, took out a bottle of vodka and two glasses.

"Vodka okay?" she said.

I smiled because I didn't know what else to do. We were having drinks like it some kind of cocktail party. Trouble was, we weren't alone. The dead were there too. She poured two drinks, then walked over to me and handed me a glass. I tried to think of an appropriate toast, but nothing came to mind. So I just knocked back half the vodka, hoping it would help.

She sipped her vodka, then looked at me.

"So what are we gonna do?" she said.

Who's we, I wanted to say. But the joke rang hollow in my throat. I searched her face for a sign, but all I saw were brown eyes deep enough to drown in, lush, full lips, and skin that looked as if she'd been airbrushed in real life. And it scared me when I realized that could be enough.

I pulled out my cellphone and punched in a number. "Hey Nic, it's me. Yeah, I know what time it is. But I need your help."

Chapter 3

An hour later a dusty black hearse that had seen better days, and maybe better corpses too, rumbled to a halt in front of the house. A funeral in the middle of the night, I thought. Down low and off the books. I saw the driver's side door swing open and went outside. A stocky black guy in his thirties wearing cargo pants and a tight afro climbed out of the hearse. He saw me and flashed an expansive smile. He was missing a couple of teeth, but I figured the gold one in front compensated for his loss.

"You McQuinn?" he said.

"Call me Max."

"I'm Ernie."

Just then a white van pulled up behind the hearse. A sign on the side read "Crime Scene Clean." The slogan beneath it said "Like It Never Happened."

Ernie glanced at the van as a white woman, thin as a rail, with a sullen face, pockmarked complexion, and a gang tattoo on her neck climbed out of the van.

"That there's Janelle," Ernie said.

Janelle ignored us and moved to the rear of the van.

"She don't talk much," Ernie said, by way of explanation. "You a friend of Rikers?"

"We have a mutual friend."

"Good to have friends when you need 'em, eh?" he said.

I nodded. "Thanks for coming out tonight."

Ernie flashed his gold tooth again. I got the feeling he was proud of it.

"No problem, man. Everybody got something to hide, right?" He scanned the front lawn. "So what we got here? I see a body over by the sign. The dude come with the house?" Then he grinned. "I'm just playin' with you, man. You got more in the house?"

I nodded. "One more."

"You the shooter?"

I shook my head, then nodded at the house. Ernie followed my line of sight and saw what I saw: Daphne standing by the window.

"She do 'em both?" Ernie said.

"Yeah, both of 'em."

"Damn," Ernie said in a hushed voice filled with awe.

"Cut the crap, Ernie," Janelle said. "We gonna do this thing or what?"

Ernie shrugged and gave me a weary smile. His burden wasn't cleaning up after the dead. It was doing it with a surly co-worker.

"On it," Ernie said.

He joined Janelle at the rear of the van. They pulled on hazmat suits, then unloaded a sprayer, scrubbing brush, wet vacuum, cleaners, solvents, disinfectants, and hazardous waste-disposal containers. They left the equipment on the ground by the van, then opened the rear door of the hearse and took out two stretchers and a pair of body bags and set them on the driveway.

"We'll move the remains first," Ernie said, "then we'll do the cleanup. Should be out of your hair in a couple hours." He nodded at the slogan on the van. "We get done, it's gonna be like it never happened. You cool with that?"

I nodded. I was cool with anything that could erase two lives, but also any evidence of their violent end. But what happened to me, was I okay with it all?

Ernie and Janelle carried a stretcher and a body bag over to where Donny lay in the grass. I watched as they placed his remains in the bag, zipped it up, then lifted the bag onto the stretcher and carried it to the hearse. They worked in silence, as if the less said the sooner it would be over. They slid the stretcher into the back, then picked up the remaining stretcher and body bag and went into the house.

I looked over at the "For Sale" sign. Even in the dark I could see the shadow of blood that had soaked into the grass. What was the plan for that, I wondered, as I waited for Ernie and Janelle to come out with Roy's body. Moments later, they did. They slid him into the hearse alongside Donny, then closed the door.

I shivered as a cold breeze swept past the house. Or maybe it was just Roy and Donny passing through on their way to eternity. I looked back at the house. Daphne was still standing by the window, watching Ernie and Janelle rewrite history. I could have gone back inside and kept her company. But I didn't want to go back in the house. Not now, not ever. It was cold outside, but I figured it would be even colder in the house.

So I shivered as I stood by the car and watched Ernie and Janelle gather up their cleaning equipment and turn their attention to removing any evidence of Roy and Donny's prior existence. Two hours later, right on schedule, they were done.

"You want to do a walk through?" Ernie asked me

after he and Janelle had loaded their equipment in the van. "Some people like to make sure we don't leave no trace."

I shook my head. "I'm good," I said.

"What about her?" Ernie said, nodding at the house. "She didn't say nothin' when we were in the house."

I turned and looked back at the house. "I think she's in shock," I said. But was I talking about Daphne, or myself?

Ernie nodded. "She'll get over it," he said.

How do you get over gunning down two men in cold blood, I wondered. But I figured Ernie knew what he was talking about. You couldn't spend your time cleaning up crime scenes without becoming some kind of expert on human nature. And maybe Daphne would get over it. And if she did, that would make it easier the next time she had to pull the trigger.

Ernie pulled off a rubber glove and we shook hands. Janelle was already back in the van, lights on, motor running. Ernie walked back to the hearse and got in behind the wheel. I heard the engine rumble to life, saw the lights come on. I realized that I hadn't even bothered to ask Ernie what they were going to do with the bodies. Maybe because I didn't want to know. I heard Daphne come up behind me as I watched the hearse and the van disappear down the dark, winding road.

"What will they do with them?" she said.

"I'm sure they'll give 'em a proper burial. They might even get some preacher to say a few words. Maybe you could send flowers."

"Stop it! You think I wanted to kill them?"

Good question, I thought. Trouble was, I didn't know the answer. All I knew is that they were dead, and

I was in the middle of it.

"You tell me, Daphne."

"I told you what happened. Why won't you believe me?"

"Because they're dead, and whether you wanted 'em dead or not doesn't much matter now. I got rid of 'em for you. Isn't that enough?"

Daphne turned and looked back at the house. "I can't stay here tonight, Max. It's like they're still here."

We got rid of the bodies and the blood, I thought, but the ghosts might decide to stick around awhile longer.

She looked up at me and even in the dark you couldn't miss those deep brown eyes. Her voice softened and she took my hand.

"Can I stay with you, just for tonight? I don't want to be alone."

****

The headlights lit up the strip of road ahead of us as we drove through the dark. Beyond that there was even more dark, and it closed in again behind us after we'd passed through it. I felt as if we were buried in the dark, that we would never drive out of it, that it would go on being dark. I glanced at Daphne. She was staring straight ahead, seeing the same thing I was, the same dark nothing, mile after mile. She must have sensed that I was looking at her because she turned to me and smiled. I didn't know what the hell there was to smile about, but I figured she was probably just being polite.

"Thanks," she said.

"For what?"

"Everything."

What did "everything" include, I wondered.

Becoming an accessory to murder? But it wasn't just me. Nicole was in deep too. What would Rikers want in return for Ernie and Janelle's services?

"Did they have families?" I said.

"Who?"

"Roy and Donny."

"I think Roy was married or something, I don't know about Donny." Then her voice sharpened. "Why'd you ask me that anyway?"

"Just habit, I guess. Writing obituaries means talking to friends and family. So I just wondered if maybe there was anyone they left behind. Must've been someone, right?"

"How the hell should I know? They tried to kill me, okay? You think they gave a shit about who I was gonna leave behind?"

I found myself wondering who Daphne would leave behind, then realized the answer was nobody because Archie was already gone.

We fell silent for a few miles as we rolled through the dark. But I knew the dark would end at some point and then I would have to figure out how to go back to the rest of my life and pretend that nothing had changed. And when I thought about that I wanted the dark to go on forever.

"They won't see anything, will they?" Daphne said, breaking the silence.

I glanced at her. "Who?"

"At the open house. They cleaned it all up, right?"

"Like it never happened."

"You sure?"

"Yeah, I'm sure," I said, as if I knew what I was talking about. She was selling a crime scene, which had to be one for the books. If she could get away with *that*, she could get away with anything.

"I need to sell it. I can't have anything else go wrong…"

I wanted to break it to her that everything had gone wrong the minute she pulled the trigger. But I was pretty sure that wasn't what she wanted to hear. So I kept the news to myself.

"I don't know what to do after," Daphne said.

"I thought you were gonna take the money and run." Then I wondered if I should run too.

"You don't understand…"

"Which part?"

"It's not over."

I took my eyes off the road for a moment, long enough to see a look on her face that scared me. "What's not over?"

"Roy and Donny weren't the only ones."

I let it sink in. It went down slow, thickening in my throat until I could scarcely breathe. By the time we got to my place in the Mission I knew the worst was on the way. And I wondered what else Daphne wasn't telling me.

"I always thought it would be fun to live in the city," she said, as she stood by my windows that looked out on Valencia Street. "But Archie didn't want neighbors. So we ended up in the hills." She turned and looked at me. "You live here alone?"

I nodded. I hadn't had a woman stay over since Sally and I split up. But I wasn't sure that Daphne counted as a sleepover. She was here for all the wrong reasons, and yet a part of me didn't want her to leave.

Daphne glanced at the wall of vinyl I'd collected

over the years and the headphones, tube amp, preamp and speakers that sat across from the records.

"I guess you like records, huh?" she said.

I nodded. "Ever since I was a kid."

"Looks like you've got the rig to play 'em too," she said, indicating the sound system. "Will you play something for me?"

I glanced at my watch. "It's the middle of the night, Daphne. I don't think my neighbors would go for it."

"I guess we better go to bed then," she said.

I knew what she meant, but for a moment I let myself believe that what she meant was we would spend the night in each other's arms. That she wanted it as much as I did. But who was I kidding? She had gunned down two men at point-blank range. I imagined if I held her close, she would smell of gunsmoke.

"I'll take the couch," I said, "you can have the bedroom."

"You sure? I don't mind the couch."

"Yeah, I'm sure," I said.

We stood in the living room like we were on a first date, neither of us knowing what our next move should be. Or maybe we knew that no matter what we did, we'd both regret it in the morning.

"I know this is awkward," Daphne said, breaking the silence. "I'll just stay tonight."

"Then what are you gonna do?"

"I don't know…go back home, get ready for the open house…"

I wondered who might show up at the open house. Would they barge in on her like Roy and Donny did? Would she have to gun them down in front of her real estate agent? Would I have to summon Ernie and Janelle, janitors of the dead, to clean up after her again? Then I realized I'd forgotten something.

"Where's the gun, Daphne?"

She looked up at me. "The gun?"

"Yeah, the gun."

"It's right here," she said, and pulled it out of her purse.

I had to admit she looked good with a gun in her hand, like she belonged on the cover of a crime novel, or maybe on TV.

"Where'd you get it?"

"It was Archie's. He kept it in the nightstand next to the bed."

"Maybe you should get rid of it," I said. "Your prints are all over it."

She gave me a look that seemed to suggest it was the dumbest idea she'd heard all day. "Why on earth would I do that?" she said. Then she offered a bitter smile. "I might need to use it again."

The way she said it, I got the feeling she couldn't wait.

"Who's coming after you next, Daphne?"

She slipped the gun back into her purse, then sank into the couch and buried her face in her hands. "You want a list?" she said, her voice muffled.

I sat down next to her and pulled her hands away from her face. She turned and looked at me. A widow with a gun in her purse and tears in her eyes.

"Archie used to brag about how it was the biggest score and nobody was ever gonna find it. A lot of people were listening."

"You can't just shoot 'em all, Daphne."

"You got a better idea?"

I didn't, and that was the problem. It was way too late to go the police. She'd be charged with murder and I'd go down as an accessory after the fact. And then they'd go after Nicole. But no matter what was going to happen, I wanted to stop thinking about it.

"Let's just get some sleep, okay? I have to go to work in the morning."

"On deadline with the dead, huh?" she said.

"Yeah, something like that," I said, wondering if I should start with Roy and Donny.

She took my hand and her warmth rushed through me like a flame. "I'm sorry I mixed you up in all this," she said softly.

"That makes two of us," I said, pulling my hand back before I got third-degree burns. Then I nodded toward the hallway off the living room. "Bedroom's down the hall on the right, across from the bathroom."

Chapter 4

When I woke up it was light out and Daphne was gone. I wondered how she managed to slip past me, seeing as how she had to get past me sprawled on the couch to reach the front door. But I guess I was out cold, which made it easy for her. Come to think of it, I was making everything easy for her. I even made it easy for her to leave without saying goodbye. She did leave me a note, though. It was on the coffee table next to my cellphone:

Thanks for letting me sleep over, Max. You're such a sweet guy. I never should have gotten you mixed up in all this, I was just scared, that's all. But I'll be okay, don't worry about me. Sorry I didn't say goodbye, just thought it would be easier this way.

Daphne

Was it easier? Maybe for her. A part of me was glad she was gone, but a bigger part wanted her to still be here. I wanted to see how she looked asleep in my bed, how she looked when she opened her eyes first thing in the morning, how she smiled when she saw I was watching her. And then what? Who was I kidding? What were we going to do after that? Go out to lunch? Plan a vacation, just the two of us? Hope the ghosts would never find us? Trouble was, the ghosts were already inside us. They would be with us wherever we went, whatever we did. Maybe Daphne knew that. Maybe that was why she was gone.

I picked up the phone and punched in her number. But all I got was voicemail, just like I knew I would. I waited for the beep, but I didn't know what to say. I could hear the rush of morning traffic on Valencia Street. I held up the phone so she could hear it too. Then I put a record on and went into the kitchen to make a pot of coffee. I had just popped a pod into the coffee maker when there was a knock at the door. Was it Daphne, I wondered. Had she changed her mind, decided she couldn't live without me? Or was it that murder was better when you could share it with a friend?

I opened the door and saw Nicole. Her face was drawn and she looked as if she'd been up half the night. Not that I could blame her. I'd made my nightmare big enough for both of us.

"Murder?" she said, a little too loud for the neighbors. "Seriously, Max? Fucking murder?"

I felt my body clench. For a minute I wondered if I was paralyzed. Then I grabbed Nicole by the arm and pulled her into the apartment before slamming the door. She stared at me, her face twisted with anger and confusion, then slumped on the couch. She buried her face in her hands.

"Could you turn off the music? No offense, but I'm not in the mood."

"Sure, no problem," I said. I went to the turntable and lifted the tonearm off the record, which continued to spin in silence.

Nic glanced at the turntable, then stood and began pacing.

"I'm sorry, Nic. I didn't know what else to do. I just figured Rikers could help."

She stopped pacing and looked at me, her eyes flashing with disbelief.

"You didn't know what to do, huh? What the fuck were you doing there in the first place? Why didn't you just walk away?"

"I've been asking myself the same question."

"It was her, right?"

I paused. What was the point of denying it when I couldn't even deny it to myself?

"Yeah, it was her."

"Unbelievable," Nicole said, sounding disgusted. "Fucking unbelievable."

She walked into the kitchen and saw the fresh cup of coffee in the machine.

"This yours?" she said.

I nodded. "Be my guest," I said.

Nicole picked up the cup and took a sip, then made a face.

"It's cold," she said, and poured the coffee out in the sink. She made herself a fresh cup, then walked over to the yellow midcentury dinette table I got on sale at an antique store on Market Street before they went out of business. She pulled out a chair and sat down, wrapped her hands around the cup and sighed. Then she looked up at me.

"I heard back from Rikers. He told me his crew cleaned up your mess."

I nodded. "Yeah, they did."

"You probably think it's over now, don't you?"

I felt my stomach tighten. "Isn't it?"

Nicole offered a bitter smile. "That's not how it works with Rikers."

I walked into the kitchen and made myself another

cup of coffee.

"How does it work?" I said, as I watched the coffee trickle into the cup.

"He did you a favor, Max."

"Tell him I appreciate it," I snapped.

I carried my cup over to the table and sat down across from Nicole. I could feel the pressure building, only I couldn't tell what it was, only where it was coming from.

Nicole paused. "You don't understand…"

"Which part," I said, sipping my coffee.

"Rikers doesn't do favors."

I looked up at her. I could see the patience in her eyes, like I was slow and she was taking her time to make sure I understood her.

"Where we going with this, Nic?"

"He wants his share."

I laughed in her face, which maybe wasn't the smartest thing to do under the circumstances. "His share? His share of what?"

"He knows all about Archie, Max, okay? How nobody knows what happened to the goods from the Paycheck Today heist."

"Right, nobody knows, Nic. Including me, his widow, and everybody else. Come on, Nic. You covered the heist. The only guy who knows is dead and buried, in case you haven't heard."

"He wants to meet tonight to discuss it."

I sat back and scoffed. "Discuss it? What are we gonna discuss, Nic?"

Nicole's eyes narrowed. I could tell she was running low on patience. "Hey!" she barked, which got my attention. "I'm in this too now, thanks to you. I'm the one who called him, okay? What do you think, you're done or something?"

I started to sweat, and I knew a shower wouldn't fix it. "I don't know anything, Nic."

I could hear myself pleading, and I hated the way it sounded.

"Ten o'clock tonight," she said.

"Where?"

"He'll let us know."

"And if we blow him off?"

Nicole shrugged. "Simple. He'll go to Dan and tell him all about it," Nicole said, referring to the detective she shared with Rikers. "You ready for that?"

"This is crazy," I said as the floor began shifting beneath my feet, shaking like an earthquake only I could feel.

Nicole leaned in and locked eyes with me. "You want to know what's crazy, Max? Crazy is you not walking away when you had the chance." She checked her watch. "Let's go, we're late for work."

I stood and it was then that the room really started moving. I grabbed the chair to steady myself and flashed on how Daphne did the same thing when she saw Roy and Donny.

Nicole must have picked up on it, because she looked over at me and said, "You okay?"

"You better drive," I said.

Chapter 5

There was a stack of manila folders on my desk when I got to the office. I knew what they were. They showed up every morning, filled with background information on obituaries that needed to be written and filed by end of day. As I settled in and switched on my computer, I wondered if the first obit I should write was my own.

Everybody wanted their cut, but at the moment their cut was one-hundred percent of nothing. But I knew that wouldn't be enough for Rikers. I figured that as far as he was concerned, somebody had to know where Archie stashed the loot. Nobody would be dumb enough to pull off a job like the Paycheck Today heist and not tell anybody about it. If only for bragging rights. All that mattered was what you believed; the truth was something that could get in the way and piss people off.

I decided I didn't feel like writing about the dead, maybe because it hit a little too close to home. I knew that the Ripper would be making his rounds, wanting to know what the lede was, when would he get the copy, was I aware of the deadlines, why was I late, the usual song and dance. But before that happened, I thought I'd refresh my memory about the Paycheck Today heist. I'd read about it when it happened, but crime wasn't my beat, so I hadn't thought much about it since. Not until Archie shuffled off and I had to write his obit. Maybe now was a good time to catch up on the one that got away.

I texted Nicole and asked her to send me the file. I could've done it myself, but it was her beat and her story, and I wanted to show respect. I also wanted her to see that I was taking the sit-down with Rikers seriously by doing my homework. But I knew the only homework that Rikers would be interested in would be the homework that pointed him to the goods. I'd get an A for that, instead of a bullet. A few minutes later, Nicole sent me the docs. I leaned into my computer and began to read.

The way Nic reported the story, a few years back Archie had gotten wind of an armored truck loaded with cash from a payday loan shark company called Paycheck Today. Nobody, including Nic, knew how exactly Archie got tipped to the cash, but to me that was the nature of his work. I figured he had people in the wind scouting for opportunities, and paid them off with a percentage of the take when the deal went down.

Archie's crew, which at the time consisted of the late Roy and Donny, were busted at the scene of the hijack. But Archie got away, just him behind the wheel of an armored truck ripe for the take. Then the truck and its contents disappeared. Roy and Donny took the fall and, absent any evidence, Archie was never charged. Nor was the take ever found. Nobody knew what happened to the take, or what was taken, or even if it had any value.

Meanwhile, back at Paycheck Today, the owner, an ex-car salesman named Vic Biderbecke, reported that he'd lost millions in the heist and filed an insurance claim. The rumor was that Biderbecke was desperate because his wife, Tiffany, had been kidnapped while on a high-priced tour of Rio and was being held for ransom.

If Vic didn't come up with the cash the kidnappers threatened to send her back in pieces via UPS or FedEx.

But the story fell apart when it was revealed that Tiffany had faked the kidnapping and planned to split the ransom with her man in Rio. As for Biderbecke, he probably should have stuck to selling cars. Insurance investigators following up on his claim discovered that he had juggled the books to support his insurance claim. Biderbecke was charged with fraud and put out of business. Plus, Tiffany, who had started at the company as a cashier and been promoted to wife, had her vacation cut short when she was extradited to the U.S. to face charges. The story ended there. Or would have ended there if it had an ending. Five years later, Archie was dead and no one knew what happened to the truck or its contents. But Roy and Donny were already dead because of it. I hoped I wasn't next on the list.

I was busy watching my life flash before my eyes when the phone rang.

"Saw Archie's obit in the paper this morning," a woman said. She sounded older, with a low, husky voice that probably sounded good over cocktails.

"Yes?"

"You wrote it, right?"

"Yes, that's right."

The call surprised me. Readers didn't often contact me directly about the obituaries that appeared under my byline. If they did have comments they usually posted them online or wrote letters to the editor. I wondered if she was a friend or maybe a family member, somebody I missed when I did my interviews.

"Max McQuinn, right?"

"Yes. What can I do for you?"

"You left something out," the woman said.

"What's that?" I said, reaching for a pen and a notepad.

"Me."

****

Scot Free Bail Bonds sat across the street from the San Francisco County Jail, a maximum-security lockup that took up the top floor of the Hall of Justice. A sign above the door read:

ALL JAILS ALL THE TIME GET OUT STAY OUT

The squat, cement-block building didn't look much bigger than a holding cell or a drunk tank. I wondered if that was a coincidence. I wasn't there to bail anybody out of jail. Not yet, anyway. But the way things were going, it could be me who needed bail. I was there to find out more about the mystery woman who had called to tell me that I had left her out of Archie's obituary. I wasn't sure what any of it had to with bail bonds, but I figured I was about to find out.

The receptionist looked up at me and gave me the once-over as I opened the door and stepped inside. She was a buxom, flaming redhead who looked to be somewhere in her fifties, and she wore gold hoop earrings and three coats of bright red lipstick.

She flashed a toothy smile filled with what appeared to be shiny new implants and said, "Hi, welcome to Scot Free Bail Bonds."

"Thanks."

"Can I help you?"

"You called me about Archie Briggs's obituary."

The smile faded. She picked up the phone and punched a number. "He's here," she said.

The door to a back office opened. A man around her age stepped out into the reception area and suddenly the room got smaller. He was big. King size. The kind of guy who took command of a room the minute he walked into it. I wondered if he'd been wrestler or a linebacker before he decided to become a bail bondsman. Though from the looks of him he could've sprung his clients from jail simply by pulling the bars apart with his bare hands. He had a silvery gray pompadour and matching mustache, and wore a sport coat, jeans, and cowboy boots.

"You the guy who wrote Archie's obit?"

"Yeah, I am."

"McQuinn, right? Max McQuinn?"

"Right."

"Benny Velasco," the man said. "Maybe you've seen my ads on TV."

"Sorry," I said, like I meant it.

He nodded at the receptionist. "This here's Ida. You left her out."

As if on cue, the corners of Ida's mouth turned down and she stuck her lower lip out.

"So I heard," I said.

"Honey, why don't you put the sign in the door," Benny said, "and we'll get comfortable in the office."

"Good idea," the receptionist said, losing the pout.

She jumped up from her desk and grabbed a sign that read "Closed, Sorry We Missed You," then walked over to the entrance. She hung the sign in the window and locked the front door, then turned back to her man.

"All set," she said with a bright smile.

All set for what, I wondered. I figured I was about to find out.

Benny extended his hand like he was an usher

showing me to my seat. "After you," he said, nodding at the back office.

"Thanks," I said, like I was grateful for the opportunity, and walked into the office.

There wasn't much to it—just a beat-up desk stacked with papers and file folders, a couple of chairs, and a love seat by the windows. I wondered if the bail bondsman and his girl used it to cuddle when business was slow. Photos of the big guy shaking hands with grateful inmates whom I assumed he'd sprung from stir were posted on the wall behind the desk. Mugshots adorned the wall across from the windows. I wasn't sure whether the mugshots matched the photos on the wall behind the desk, but I got the message. First they were stuck behind bars and then they were out, thanks to the big guy at Scot Free Bail Bonds.

"Have a seat," the big guy said, pointing to one of the chairs facing the desk.

I sat down, relieved he didn't point at the loveseat. Ida sat down next to me and Benny pulled back his desk chair and joined us.

"I guess you're probably wondering why we called you down here," Benny said as he swung his feet up onto his desk. His boots were king size, just like the rest of him.

I cocked my head at the woman sitting next to me. "You said I left her out of the obituary."

"Yeah, you did, and here's why that matters—"

"Benny, honey," Ida said, "could we just back up here for a minute?"

"Sure, no problem, pumpkin," Benny said with a tight smile.

She smiled at me like I was lost. "The poor man

doesn't even know what's he's doing here," Ida said.

I smiled politely and hoped she didn't want to take me home.

"We wanted to fill you in on what the bitch didn't tell you."

I whipped around to Ida. "Excuse me?" I said, with what I assumed was a startled look on my face.

"Daphne Swan," Benny said. "She didn't tell you, did she?"

"Tell me what?" I wondered what else Daphne was supposed to tell me, and why I was finding out about it from other people.

"I was Archie's first wife," Ida said. "Married him back in '99."

I stared at her, stunned by the news, and tried to imagine her and Archie together twenty-five years ago. But it didn't work because all I saw was Daphne.

"His first wife?"

Ida offered me a knowing smile. "You didn't know about me, did you?"

I shook my head. "No, I didn't."

"She didn't tell you 'cause she wants to keep it all for herself," Ida said.

Benny swung his feet back onto the floor. His boots landed with a thud that shook the building.

"That shit ain't gonna fly with me and Ida."

So that was it. The happy couple wanted their cut. Then I remembered what Daphne told me. Roy and Donny weren't the only ones.

"So where the fuck is it?" Ida said, her voice cold as a cop shaking down a suspect.

"Where's what?"

"Don't play frickin' dumb with us, sonny," Benny

said.

"I don't know what you're talking about."

I knew damn well what they were talking about, but it was the last thing I wanted to know. Roy and Donny wanted to know, and look what it got them.

"Like hell you don't."

"Where's the fucking money?" Benny said. "The Paycheck Today job. I got to spell it out for you?"

"You do know about the Paycheck Today job, don't you?" Ida said.

"Yeah, I heard about it. So have a lot of other people. But that's all I know, okay?"

Benny leaned in and looked at me. "But Daphne knows all about it, right? So what'd she tell you?"

"She said Archie never told her what he did with the money."

Benny and Ida exchanged glances.

"Next you're gonna tell us you believe her, right?" Ida said.

I wasn't sure who or what I believed anymore, but I was pretty sure that Daphne Swan wasn't at the top of the list of people I would call believable.

"Doesn't matter whether I believe her or not."

"Is that right?" Benny said, like he wasn't happy to hear it.

"Yeah, that's right. I write obituaries, I don't solve mysteries."

Benny scraped back his chair and stood, and suddenly the room got smaller. Or maybe it was just me.

"Well, you gonna have to solve this one, sonny," he said, "and I mean sooner rather than later." He nodded at Ida. "This little lady been waiting too long for what's hers, and you're gonna make sure she gets it."

"I got it coming, okay?" Ida said, just in case I hadn't gotten the message. "I don't care if he's dead, the sonofabitch still owes me!"

"Why me? You want to know what Daphne knows about the Paycheck Today job, why don't you go ask her?"

Benny shook his head. "She won't talk to us," he said, "but she already talked to you."

"She talked to me about Archie. She didn't talk to me about the Paycheck Today job."

Benny flashed a genial smile. "So now the two of you are gonna keep talking, and the way I figure it, sooner or later she's gonna tell you all about it."

I shook my head. I was already in deep; I didn't need to get buried alive. "Sorry, wish I could help you, but I've already got a day job." I glanced at my watch but didn't catch the time. But I was already late, maybe too late. "And you know what? I'm on deadline."

Benny lost the smile. "I don't give a fuck about your deadline. You're gonna find out what she knows, you hear me?" He nodded at the photos on the wall. "You see these pictures? You know why these folks look so happy?"

"Benny did 'em a favor," Ida said. "He got 'em out of jail. That's how come they're happy."

"That's right, I did 'em a favor. Which means they owe me one. So if I was to need some help making sure that you find out what I need to know, I might have to call in a favor. You catch my drift?"

I looked up at the photos. They did look happy, no question about it. Would they be happy to push me around as a favor to the man to whom they owed their freedom? I didn't want to find out. But I also wasn't sure how I was going to get Daphne to suddenly remember what she didn't know. I used to think the dead were easy to work with, but Archie Briggs had proved me wrong.

"I'll see what I can do," I said, hoping that would be enough to get me out of the office in one piece.

Benny flashed his genial smile again. "There you go," he said. "That wasn't so hard, was it?"

"Don't be a stranger now," Ida said with a smile.

Fat chance of that I thought, as I brushed past her on my way to the door.

Chapter 6

I felt as if I was out on bail. I wondered if maybe I should send Benny a headshot that he could add to his gallery of grateful cons. But I knew that he didn't want a headshot, he wanted the loot, and if I didn't deliver he'd forfeit my bail. I wanted to say why me, but why bother? I already knew why. I had written Archie's obit, which, ironically, had brought him back to life and reminded everybody of the Paycheck Today heist. Somehow, because I'd managed to summon Archie back from the grave, everybody assumed he'd told me where the money was. It didn't make any sense, but neither did me posing as a cross between a medium and a private detective. I didn't know anything about the heist, but that didn't matter. All that mattered was what people believed. And that was why I was out on bail.

The Ripper was waiting for me when I got to the office. I thought I saw his face brighten at the sight of me, and it worried me. Dickie's face never brightened, unless of course he was about to go in for the kill.

"I noticed you didn't clean out your desk, so I assumed you were coming back," Dickie said, looking around my cubicle. I noticed that he was holding a manila folder.

"Sorry, I just lost track of the time."

"I'll tell you what else you lost track of, Max. Deadlines. You remember deadlines, mate?"

How could I forget? I lived and breathed deadlines eight hours a day, five days a week. I'd lost track of how many souls had passed through my hands on their way to eternity. The dead were my life. But I never thought, as I did now, that they might kill me.

The Ripper slapped the manila folder on my desk. "You're gonna love this one," he said.

"Great," I said, not knowing what else to say.

"Guess who's dead?" he said, like he was excited about it.

"I give up."

"Remember Vic Biderbecke?"

The name did more than ring a bell. It made me think of Daphne.

"How could I forget?" I said. "The Paycheck Today job."

"Weird coincidence, huh? First Archie and then Vic." Dickie looked up at the ceiling, as if seeking guidance from a higher authority. "They're probably up there right now, arguing over the take."

Biderbecke had staged the heist to try and ransom his wife Tiffany, not knowing that she'd faked her kidnapping while on vacation and was planning to split the take with her man in Rio. But the scheme fell apart when investigators took a closer look, and both Vic and Tiffany wound up in prison. Not exactly what they had in mind, but that was the thing about life—it was never about you.

"So what happened?" I said.

"Got himself killed in a prison riot. Go figure, huh?"

"What about Tiffany?"

"Still in prison, as far as I know." He nodded at the manila folder. "Be sure to work that in. Give the lede some color, you know what I mean? Something like 'Jailed prison wife mourns double-crossed ex.'"

That was the Ripper, always looking for the tabloid angle. He missed his calling, I thought, but then again, maybe so did I.

"Maybe you could go talk to her," he said.

I looked up at him, surprised by the suggestion. "Tiffany?"

"Yeah, why not? You might learn something."

That was what I was afraid of, I thought. I'd learned enough already. Maybe more than enough. But all I said was, "Sure, no problem."

Dickie grinned. "That's what I like to hear, 'no problem'. Keep me posted." Then he turned and walked away.

I watched him make his way across the newsroom to his office. Don't ask me why I was watching Dickie. It wasn't like there was anything special about watching a skinny, middle-age white guy walk across a newsroom. In fact, it was pretty ordinary, mundane even. But maybe mundane and ordinary were what I needed at the moment. My cellphone pinged with a text from Nicole. I didn't have to read it to know that mundane and ordinary were not in the cards.

Nicole:—*We're on for tonight. Stay tuned.*—
****

I was sitting in the car, waiting for rush hour traffic to clear so I could pull out of the parking garage without getting T-boned when I saw her. Or I guess I should say I saw the car. Daphne's cherry red convertible. The top was down and Daphne was in the car. But she wasn't behind the wheel. Some kid was doing the driving for her. I only caught a glimpse of him as the car rolled past me, but he had blond hair and looked like a surfer who'd traded in his board for a ragtop.

Who was he, I wondered, and what was he was doing driving her car. But there was more to it than that. I guess what I really wanted to know was, what he was doing with her in the first place. I didn't want to admit that I was jealous. How could I be jealous when I barely knew her? Then again, I knew her well enough to help her cover up a double homicide. I figured that should count for something. But seeing as how she hadn't returned my calls, I guess it didn't count for much. All that mattered was that he was in the car with her and I wanted to know why. Why did I want to know? Simple. She was in my head, whether I liked it or not.

I hesitated for a moment, as if to consider whether my next move made any sense. Then, as the oncoming traffic caught a light at the intersection, I pulled out and followed them. It didn't make sense, but nothing had made sense since the day I met her. The streets were thick with commuters trying to get home, but it was still daylight and the ragtop stood out in a sea of cars that all looked alike. So did Daphne. I tailed them through the Mission, then up to the Financial District, and tried to imagine where they were going. I had no idea, of course. But that didn't stop me from thinking about it, perhaps because it was the only thing on my mind. Thanks to Daphne, I had managed to forget that Nic and I had a date with Rikers to find out what he wanted in exchange for the clean-up crew that made a crime scene look like it never happened.

Then I noticed that the car's right taillight was blinking. The car slowed as the surfer moved into the right lane, then pulled into a parking space in front of a bank. A uniformed security guard was standing by the entrance, next to a sign that said the bank was open until six at night. Daphne and the surfer left the top down as they got out of the car and walked into the bank. At least they weren't holding hands, I thought, as I parked in a loading zone and watched the front door close behind them. What were they doing in a bank, I wondered. I knew that Daphne was hard up for money, but what did that have to do with the guy behind the wheel? My mind raced with questions I had no business asking and no way of answering.

I was still watching the bank, acting as if I was waiting for Daphne to come out and explain it all to me, when my cellphone rang.

"We're going to a movie," Nicole said, cutting to the chase.

Chapter 7

It was grindhouse night at the Roxie, a San Francisco revival house on 16th Street in the Mission. Nic and I got there just in time for a midnight screening of "Ilsa: She Wolf of the SS," a seventies exploitation flick about a horny, sadistic Nazi prison commandant. The posters in the lobby screamed "The Most Dreaded Nazi of Them All!" and "She Committed Crimes So Terrible Even the SS Feared Her!"

I wasn't sure what Ilsa had to do with payback for the clean-up crew at Daphne's house, but this was Rikers' party, not mine.

"Your guy into this stuff?" I said, nodding at the posters.

Nic shrugged. "Does it matter?"

I opened the door to the auditorium, then turned to her. "I'm sorry about all this, Nic." It sounded lame, but I didn't know what else to say.

"Sorry, huh? I guess that makes it all better, right?"

She brushed past me and I followed her into the darkened auditorium.

"You see him?" I said.

"I can't see anything yet."

"Right."

A trailer for a movie about some women in prison was on the screen. I figured it was the warm-up act for Ilsa.

"He's over there," Nic said after her eyes had adjusted to the dark.

I followed her line of sight and saw a skinhead sitting in the back row on the other side of the nearly deserted theater.

"After you," I said.

We made our way across the auditorium. Rikers glanced at us as we approached him. Up close he looked like a greasy street rat in his thirties, with pale skin and a face that was plowed with scars, as if the knives had been out for him since the day he was born. The shadow of a gang tattoo peeked out of the frayed collar of his hoodie.

A thin smile spread across his narrow, bony face. "Hey Nic, glad you could make it."

"Did we have a choice?"

Rikers ignored the question. He looked past her and saw me. "I see you brought a date."

I said nothing, just stared at him in the dark. I was standing with my back to the screen when I heard the movie start. But I didn't bother turning around. I had a feeling I'd seen it all before.

"Let's get to it," Nicole said. "We don't have all night."

"Sure, no problem." He nodded at the empty seats next to him. "Have a seat, let's talk."

Nicole and I sat down next to him. The seat was cramped and the upholstery was worn and stained. I noticed that somebody had stuck a stick of gum on the seatback in front of me. Suddenly, I just wanted to get whatever the hell it was over with.

"Okay, we're all sitting down," I said. "What do you want?"

"You're McQuinn, right?" Rikers said. "Max

McQuinn?"

I nodded. "Yeah, that's right."

Rikers stuck out his hand. I pretended not to see it. I didn't need to shake hands with the guy who was shaking me down.

He shrugged it off and let his hand drop on the arm rest. "I hear Ernie and Janelle cleaned it all up for you. Like it never happened, right?"

"That's why we're here, isn't it?"

"We all know why we're here," Nic said sharply. "So let's get it over with."

She wanted to leave as badly as I did. She'd reached out to Rikers for help and probably regretted it ever since. She wasn't the only one.

"What's the rush, Knickers?" Rikers said. "You always got time for me when you want a tip."

Nicole scowled. "Don't call me that!"

"Hey, I'm just playin' with you, girl, you know that."

"This some kind of game to you?" I said.

"It's all a game, man. All that matters is whether you're winning or losing. I helped you win with the clean-up, right? Now I get to win."

"So what do you want, a piece of Archie's score?"

Rikers flashed a dirty smile that degenerated into a leer. "I want a piece of her."

Nicole and I exchanged glances. I figured the shocked expression on her face matched my own.

I looked at Rikers and said, "Excuse me?"

I wanted to pretend that maybe I hadn't heard right. That maybe I'd misunderstood him because of the sounds of the prisoners rioting onscreen.

"Daphne Swan," Rikers said.

I could feel the rage building inside, the heat rising up until it seemed as if every part of me was on fire. Nicole must've sensed that I was about to lunge at him, because as I rose up out of my seat, she put her arm out to stop me.

"You're disgusting," she said.

"Yeah, until you need me."

"We look like pimps to you?"

Rikers shrugged. "I don't fuckin' care what you look like. That's what I got coming, and that's what I want."

I scoffed. "Dream on, asshole. It's never gonna happen."

Rikers scowled at me, then looked at Nicole. "It better happen, 'cause if it don't, our friend's gonna hear about what went down up at her house."

I knew that the "friend" Rikers was referring was Dan Bellamy, Nicole's ex and the SFPD detective with whom she shared Rikers as a CI. I also knew that Nicole wasn't happy to have their relationship thrown back in her face. Maybe it wasn't a good idea to mix business with pleasure.

"Is that some kind of threat?"

"Fuck yeah, it's a threat. I helped you out." His eyes darted from Nicole to me, then back again. "You don't help me out…"

His voice trailed off. He didn't need to finish the sentence. Nicole and I both knew what he meant. I felt sick inside. I didn't care about the money. If Archie's score ever turned up, I'd be happy to give him a piece of it. But a piece of Daphne?

"You sent them up there," Nicole said. "You're just as guilty as we are. If we go down, you go down with us."

Rikers shrugged. "You think Dan's gonna let that happen to his favorite snitch?"

Nicole locked eyes with Rikers. "You want to take that chance?"

"Do you?"

Nicole held his gaze for a moment longer, then looked away.

"We're done here," she said, and stood. Then she turned to me. "You ready?"

I nodded and stood up.

"You guys leaving already?" Rikers said. He nodded at the screen. "The movie's not over."

"Stay the fuck away from her," I said.

Rikers gave me a cold smile. "You want to go down for the guys she clipped? The bitch worth that much to you?"

I gave myself a moment to think about it as the screen roared with Nazi prison mayhem. But I didn't need a moment. Truth was, I didn't need any time at all. I lunged at Rikers and grabbed him by the collar and pulled him up out of his seat. He glared at me, but I could see he was scared too.

"Max! Stop!" Nicole said, as she tried to pull me away from Rikers. "Let him go!"

"Shut the fuck up!" a patron shouted from somewhere in the dark.

"Max!"

I held onto Rikers for a moment longer, long enough for him to know that I liked seeing the fear in his eyes, then dropped him back into his seat.

"Can we go now, please," Nicole said, "before somebody calls the police?"

I nodded and we edged our way down the row

toward the center aisle.

"You're gonna regret this!" Rikers shouted at us as we walked out of the auditorium.

I already did, I thought, more than you know.

It felt good to be outside. A midnight wind was blowing down Valencia, and it made me want to stand in the middle of the street with my arms outstretched like some kind of Christ and let it blow through me until I felt pure again.

I had expected Rikers to add his name to the list of creditors who seemed to think that Archie owed them a piece of his legendary score. But Rikers didn't want a piece of Archie's score—he wanted to score with Daphne. I tried to imagine how I was supposed to make that happen. What was I, a middleman, a pimp, a go-between? I felt like I needed a shower after Rikers. I also knew that I could not let him touch her, no matter what it cost me. But what if the price was too high? Was I willing to take the fall for Roy and Donny's murders? Would Daphne and I hold hands all the way to the prison gates, then promise to write forever after?

The marquee had gone dark but Nic and I were still standing on the sidewalk in front of the theater. It hit me that we looked like a couple trying to decide where to grab a drink before last call. But Nicole had something else on her mind.

"We have to get rid of him," she said, her voice as cold as the breeze whipping past us.

I looked at her. "Get rid of him? What are you talking about?"

"You heard me."

"That's nuts."

"Is it? He doesn't want the money, he wants her.

And what do you think is gonna happen after that? He's gonna want more of her. Where's it end, Max? You started this, tell me how it ends."

"Nic, listen to yourself. We covered up two murders. You want to cover up another one? Don't we have enough blood on our hands already?"

"We wouldn't be covering up anything if you'd stayed out of it," Nicole said sharply.

I said nothing. I'd had the same conversation with myself ever since it happened.

Nicole paused, then said, "She can do it."

I looked at her. "Daphne?"

"She did the other two. She can do him too. What's one more?"

"What's one more? It's murder, that's what it is."

"She'll probably be happy to do it once she finds out he wants to fuck her. Anyway, you got a better idea?"

I didn't and she knew it. She turned and headed down the street.

I called after her. "Nic, wait a minute, where you going?"

"Home."

"Don't you want a ride?"

"No," came her voice from the dark.

And then I was alone.

I sat in the car and waited for my life to flash before my eyes. But it didn't happen. Whatever life I'd lived so far was gone and the rest was about to go up in smoke. Nic was furious with me for getting her mixed up in a double murder, and now she wanted to make it a triple. A home run, I guess you could call it. All it took for her to change her mind was ten minutes in the dark with Rikers. But didn't she know going in what he was?

Hadn't she used him again and again to scoop news stories? He was a snitch, a rat, a spy who informed on other people for his own advantage. And maybe because he got off on it. And now he wanted to get off with Daphne.

I started the car and switched on the headlights. The beams lit up the street in front of me, but I still couldn't see where I was going. Or maybe I just didn't want to look. I caught a light a few blocks away and texted Nic to make sure she was okay. But she never got back to me. The night seemed to get darker as I drove home, and I felt as if I was losing her along with everything else in my life. All because I didn't walk away when I should have. And now, instead of walking away from trouble, I was running toward it, as if I couldn't wait to dive head first into the deep end.

****

I was almost home when I realized that I didn't want to be alone with myself. I checked my watch. Last call was an hour away. Maybe if I was lucky I could catch the last set at Bird's. Named in honor of Charlie Parker, whose nickname was Yardbird, Bird's was a basement dive on lower Fillmore. The club had been around for years, and back in the day it showcased all the top players. But over time the stars moved on, and now Bird's was the best place to hear local talent and players you never heard of, which I figured was a pretty good way to keep jazz alive.

When I pulled up in front of the club, I noticed that the sign above the awning that spelled "Bird's" was missing a couple of lights. I wondered if the club was falling on hard times or just short of bulbs. The club was opened back in the Fifties by a guy named Jimmie and his wife Alberta. The timing was right, and for the first few years the joint was jumping.

But things took a serious turn for the worse when Jimmie got himself shot by his mistress. She clipped him one night while he was tending bar, filling in for the regular guy who'd gotten pinched on a parole beef. After that, the club changed hands a number of times over the years, and I didn't know who owned it now. But it still was what it was always was, a blues and jazz dive where passions ran high, and anything could happen before last call. Maybe that was why I was there.

A white piano player, a brunette on tenor, a black drummer who never took off his shades, and a skinny Asian cat who played bass were onstage, playing the kind of West Coast cool you wanted to hear after midnight. I headed over to the bar and grabbed an empty stool.

The redhead behind the bar glanced at me and smiled. She was in her thirties, and she rocked a butch haircut and a nose ring, jeans, and black Bird's T-shirt.

"Hey Max, what you doin' out on a school night?"

"One of those nights, I guess, Jane," I said.

Jane pouted. "And here I thought it was because you wanted to see me."

I smiled. I knew she was kidding, but I also knew she wasn't kidding. Jane and I had hooked up a few times, but we'd never managed to make it more than that, even though we belonged to the same tribe. Which meant Jane liked hanging out and playing records as much as I did. I couldn't remember exactly why we didn't work out, but then I couldn't recall much about the women in my life before Daphne. They were all in a kind of fog, and the only one I could see clearly right now was

Daphne.

"I didn't know you'd be working tonight."

"Of course not. How could you?"

"But I'm glad you are," I said. "It's really good to see you."

"Yeah? No weird old girlfriend vibe?"

I smiled and shook my head. "Not a chance."

"What's it like then, Max? Old times?"

I looked up at her and our eyes met. For a moment I saw the flash of a life that might have been possible. I held her gaze until she looked away and glanced at the stage.

"These cats are good, aren't they?"

"Yeah, they are," I said, as the moment passed.

"So, what can I get you? Vodka tonic, right?"

I nodded. "You remembered."

"Yeah, I remembered," Jane said with a rueful smile.

She turned away to make my drink. Then a few other patrons sidled up to the bar and it wasn't just the two of us anymore.

"Here you go," Jane said, as she set my drink in front of me. "See you around, I guess, huh?" She tried to make it sound casual, but we both knew better.

Then she moved away from me. I could hear the other people at the bar shouting out their orders over the sound of the band. I sipped my drink slowly and let the music I'd loved since I was a kid wash over me. Maybe if I listened long enough the music could drown out the murderous tune in my head.

Chapter 8

The next morning, I swung by Nic's cubicle as soon as I got in, but she was on the phone and waved me off. I thought she might come by after she got off, but she never did. I wondered if maybe she was trying to forget that we had talked about murder the night before. Not that I could blame her. I was doing my best to forget it too, but it wasn't working. The thought of killing Rikers was in my head, like a gun waiting to go off. Still, it wasn't like Nic to just blow me off. Then again, maybe neither one of us was the same person we were before Daphne pulled the trigger.

I didn't hear back from Nic, but I did hear from the Ripper. He reminded me that Vic Biderbecke's obit was pending, and that I needed to get my ass out to Santa Rita and score an interview with his widow sooner rather than later.

An hour later I headed out to Santa Rita Jail in Dublin, thirty miles away. After being processed into the facility as a visitor, I was directed to Tiffany Biderbecke's housing unit. I could hear the prison soundtrack ringing in my ears as I walked across the landscaped grounds—the blare of TVs, inmates shouting and cursing, alarms going on and off, the echo of cell doors slamming shut.

Being in jail wasn't just about being trapped in a cage in hell. It was about being trapped in a cage with constant, desperate, violent noise roaring all around you. And at Santa Rita, there was plenty of noise to go around. It was the third-largest jail in California, with thirty-five housing units and up to 4,000 prisoners. I didn't know whether the jail was at capacity or maybe over capacity, like so many other prisons, but I figured they could always make room for a washed-up obituary writer who didn't know when to quit. Then I could be trapped in my own private hell. But the way things were going I felt as if I was already there.

I stepped into the housing unit and showed a guard my visitor's pass. He sent me down a long corridor that led to the visiting room. The air was thick with the smell of disinfectant, and the signs on the walls warned that any violation of visitation policy would result in immediate expulsion or arrest. The visiting room itself was shaped like a shoebox and smelled like one too. A row of booths had been squeezed into the box, and they were filled with female inmates on one side and friends and loved ones on the other.

Bulletproof glass ran the length of the box, separating the guests of Alameda County from those who came to visit them. Dull black wall phones that never rang hung on both sides of the booths, and the glass was smeared with handprints. The inmates were seated on stainless steel stools behind the glass barrier, and they were anxiously scanning the faces of the visitors who were entering the room.

Tiffany was one of them. I recognized her from her mugshot. Her face was pale and her hair was dull, as if prison had taken the life out of her. Like all the other inmates, she was wearing a blue jumpsuit. She watched me with sullen eyes as I scraped back the chair and sat down. Then she picked up the phone and I did likewise.

"McQuinn?" she said.

I nodded. "Yeah, Max McQuinn, *Bay Area Bugle*."

"What do you want?"

"I wanted to talk about Vic."

"Vic's dead."

"Yeah, I know. I'm writing his obituary."

Tiffany offered a scornful smile. "No shit, he gets an obituary, huh?"

"I thought maybe there might be something you'd want people to know about him."

"Seriously?"

I nodded. "Yeah, seriously."

Tiffany looked down at her chipped fingernails. "He never came to see me. Didn't write neither. I guess he never got over it."

"It?"

"You know, the kidnapping and stuff."

"Was it your idea?"

She looked up at me. "The kidnapping?"

"Yeah."

Tiffany nodded. "Me and this guy I met in Rio…we kinda came up with it together." She gave a wry smile. "Seemed like a good idea at the time."

"You ever hear from him, the guy in Rio?"

Tiffany shook her head. "We lost touch after I got sent back to the States. Could be in jail like me for all I know."

"Got any ideas on what happened to the money?"

"What money?"

"The Paycheck Today heist."

"You mean Archie's heist?"

"Yeah."

"I don't know nothin' about that. I thought you were talking about the ransom."

I looked up at her, surprised. "Vic paid it?"

"Fuck yeah, he paid it, but me and Ronaldo never got it."

"Why not?"

"Rio cops grabbed it just before we got busted. Somebody tipped 'em, I guess."

"Got any idea who?"

Tiffany gave a helpless shrug. "Beats me. Next thing I knew we were in handcuffs." She paused, as if to let the memory linger, then changed the subject. "They knew each other, you know, from the old days."

I felt another jolt of surprise. "Vic and Archie?"

"Yeah, back when Vic was a loan shark, before he went legit."

"You think they set it up?"

"The heist?"

I nodded.

"Maybe. Hard to say since nobody knows what happened to it."

"What about the people who worked in the office?"

"What about them?"

"You think maybe they might know something about it?"

Tiffany shrugged. "If they did, they didn't tell me nothin' about it."

"What if I wanted to talk to 'em? You got any names?"

Tiffany gave me a sly smile. "You writing Vic's obit or looking for the money?"

A buzzer sounded. Visiting hours were over. As if on cue, a guard stepped forward.

"Time's up, Biderbecke," she said.

"You could talk to Cathy Wu, if you can find her," Tiffany said, ignoring the guard. "She was Vic's office manager when they shut him down."

"Let's go," the guard said.

"Wait a minute," Tiffany said, trying to shake her off.

"Now," the guard said firmly.

"You gonna put me in his obit?" Tiffany said with a teasing smile as the guard pulled her to her feet. "Don't call me Biderbecke, baby. Call me Tiffany."

I smiled. She was some kind of star, if only to herself. But maybe that was enough to get by in a place like this. All around me, inmates and visitors were holding their palms up to the glass and saying goodbye. Smearing their fingerprints on top of all the others who had come and gone and would come again. I could hear people crying and sniffling, the sound of chairs scraping concrete. A moment later, Tiffany joined the shuffling parade of inmates filing out of the visiting room.

Traffic was heavy back to the city, and by the time I got to the office it was late afternoon. Time was running out and I was still on deadline for Vic Biderbecke's obit. But now that Tiffany had given me Cathy Wu's name, I wanted to talk to her before we went to press. I wasn't sure what she could add to the obit, but writing obituaries meant talking to as many people as possible who knew the deceased. Wu not only knew Vic, but she also worked for him, ran the Paycheck Today office. Did she know something about the heist? No harm in asking.

On a hunch that she still worked in the same industry, I made a list and started working the phone, calling around to other payday loan stores in the Bay

Area. I was halfway down the list and tired of people telling me they never heard of her when I got lucky. She was working as a cashier for an outfit in the South Bay called Payday Everyday. She was about to leave for the day when I reached her, but she gave me her cellphone number and told me to call her in the car. We could chat while she drove to her Pilates class. It was illegal in California to use a cellphone while driving, but since I didn't exactly have the law on my side, I kept it to myself and hoped she didn't get pulled over.

"What happened?" she said, when I told her Vic was dead.

"He was killed in a prison riot."

"How awful. I felt so bad when he was convicted…it was like a double whammy."

"How do you mean?"

"First, Tiffany scammed him, and then the government sent him to prison."

"Did you know it was a scam at the time?"

"No, he played it pretty close to the vest. I didn't know what was going on until he got busted."

"I imagine he must've been pretty upset about the heist."

"You know, it was a funny thing, he seemed more upset about how Tiffany had cheated on him and betrayed him."

"She told me Vic and Archie Briggs knew each other."

"You saw her?"

"Yeah, I did."

"Is she still in prison?"

"Yeah, she is."

"She really screwed him over, her and her Brazilian

65

boyfriend."

"Was she right about Vic and Archie?"

"Yeah, they did know each other. Archie used to come by the office sometimes."

"Do you suppose he knew about the heist?"

"Maybe. I mean, that was his line of work, right? But you want to hear something funny?"

"Sure," I said. The way things were going, I could use a laugh.

"Just before it happened, Vic ordered a big supply of play money."

"Play money?" I said, surprised by the news.

"Yeah, tons of it in hundred-dollar bills."

"Why?"

"I have no idea. Weird, huh?"

"Yeah, weird. What happened to it?"

"The play money?"

"Yeah."

"Disappeared."

I was still trying to wrap my head around why a guy who dealt in real money wanted play money when Wu interrupted my thoughts.

"Listen, I hate to cut this short, but I'm at my class."

"Sure, no problem," I said, "thanks for your time."

I didn't know what I would learn about Vic before I spoke to Cathy Wu, but I never imagined it would've been play money. That was the thing about interviewing friends, family, and associates of the deceased. They all revealed different sides of a person, like a hall of mirrors that kept reflecting different versions, and left you wondering which one was real. When it came to Vic Biderbecke, the only thing I knew was real was that he was dead.

I stayed after hours to knock out a draft of Vic's obit, then sent it to the Ripper. I even used his headline— 'Jailed Prison Wife Mourns Double-Crossed Ex'— which I figured would make his day. But the whole time I was writing it I couldn't help wondering if it should have been a double obit for Vic and Archie. It wasn't just because they both had shuffled off at the same time. That was just coincidence, and sometimes death was like that. It was more about the questions that occurred to me after Tiffany revealed that they knew each other back in the day before Vic went legit.

Now I wondered what else they had in common. If Archie's heist was a setup, what happened to the loot? Was it part of the plan to have it disappear? Or did it all go south for some reason? And what about the ransom money? Who tipped the Rio cops about it? And how did they know that Tiffany's kidnapping was a scam? Was it Archie? And if it was Archie, why did he turn on Vic and Tiffany? And what about Daphne? She had to know more than she was letting on, but how much more? And what about the play money? Why did Vic want it, and what did he plan to do with it?

My mind raced with questions searching for answers, but no matter how many times I asked myself the questions, I was never able to answer them. Instead, they led to even more questions, and after a while I just got dizzy thinking about it all. I was an obituary writer, not a detective. And yet, here I was, trying to interview the past to make sense of the present. Then again, maybe it was too late to make sense of anything. I was in deep, and that never made sense.

Then my cellphone pinged with a text. I glanced at the screen and saw it was from Nicole.

—I'm at Dewey's. We need to talk.—

Chapter 9

The happy hour crowd had moved on by the time I got to Dewey's, and the drunks who were left behind were still trying to get there, one drink at a time. I saw Nicole sitting at a table in the back, across from the neon Miller High Life sign and next to the cigarette machine. A drink sat on a cocktail napkin in front of her. I noticed that there was another drink in front of the empty seat across from her. I figured that one was mine. She'd apparently assumed I'd need a drink, and had taken the liberty of ordering for me. She was right. I did need a drink. Maybe more than one.

I scraped back the chair and sat down. "Thanks," I said, nodding at the drink in front of me.

Nicole smiled. "I hate drinking alone."

She picked up her drink. I did likewise. We clinked glasses, then sipped our drinks. It was the best thing I'd tasted all day.

"I'm sorry about last night," Nic said.

"Which part?"

"I shouldn't have walked away like that."

"Yeah, you're right."

"I just couldn't talk about it then, all I could do was just tell you what we had to do, just so you'd know."

"Right. So I could be up all night thinking about it."

"I was up all night with it too, Max."

"And then you came to your senses and couldn't

wait to tell me, right?"

Nic paused. Her hands tightened around her glass. Then she looked up at me and my heart sank. It was as if I knew what she was going to say before she said it. But then she said it anyway.

"I meant what I said, Max."

I shook my head. "That's great, Nic. Congratulations."

Nicole frowned. "Spare me the sarcasm, okay?"

"Nic, help me out here. You freaked out when you found out about Roy and Donny. You told me I should've walked away. You remember that?"

"Yeah, I remember."

"And now you want to join the club? What the fuck happened to you?"

"I know him, Max. He'll take us down. He'll go to Dan, and he'll get off on it. I never should've asked for his help in the first place."

"Yeah, and I never should've asked you for help."

"Whatever. Now he's got us, don't you see?"

I gulped my drink, then set my glass down harder than I should have. Some of the booze splashed onto the table, which I regretted, because I would have preferred to drink it.

"I'll tell you what I see," I said. "I see two people making a big mistake. And I already made a big mistake. And you know what really scares me, Nic? I think you really mean it."

Nic leaned in and locked eyes with me. "Why should we go down for Roy and Donny? We didn't shoot 'em; she did. Anyway, nobody likes a snitch, Max. They're rats, and nobody's gonna miss a rat when he's gone."

"What about all the scoops you got from him, Nic? You gonna miss that?"

Nicole stiffened. "I got the scoops, okay? Last time I checked his name wasn't on the byline."

"What about Dan? What's he gonna do when his snitch turns up dead?"

Nicole shrugged. "Same thing I'm gonna do. Find another one."

I knocked back what was left of my drink, which wasn't enough. Maybe it was the crime beat, I thought, that made Nicole want to take a chance on life outside the law. I covered the dead, but that didn't make me want to be dead. Crime was different. Crime was about what you could get away with. Had her years of reporting on crimes and the criminals who committed them make her think that we could get away with it? Or was she just too scared of what might happen if we blew Rikers off? I was scared either way, so maybe in the end it was a matter of what we could live with, and whether we thought we could get away with it.

"So what are you gonna do, Max?" Nic said, interrupting my thoughts. "Pimp out Daphne, or put a gun in her hand?"

Maybe both, I thought. Then I flagged a bartender and ordered another round.

I couldn't stop driving after I left the bar. Even though I'd had way too much to drink. Because if I stopped driving then I would have start thinking, and that was the last thing I wanted to do. And so I kept moving, going nowhere in the dark because it was the only place I felt safe. I headed out of the city, across the Bay Bridge to Oakland, and from there down Interstate 880 toward the airport. As I passed Oakland International, I caught sight of a jetliner taking altitude, and thought about catching a flight to a place I'd never been just so I could say I was somewhere else. But then I figured that everything I was trying to drive away from would be waiting for me when I got off the plane, along with the jetlag.

And so instead of catching a flight I took the San Mateo Bridge back across the bay and headed north toward the city. Then my cellphone rang and I saw it was her. I wondered if the gun was still in her purse. Then I remembered what she said when I told her she should get rid of it.

Why on earth would I do that? I might need to use it again.

"Hey, stranger," I said. "You get my messages?"

"Sorry, I should've called you back sooner."

"Why didn't you?"

"I just felt bad, getting you mixed up in all this. I never wanted that to happen."

"It's a little late for that now."

"I don't want it to get any worse."

"It always gets worse, Daphne."

Daphne fell silent. I wondered if she'd just faded away as easily as she'd faded in, a voice drifting in and out of the dark.

"So why you calling me now?" I said, just to make sure she was still there.

"I'm scared, Max."

You're not the only one, baby, I thought. But what was the point of telling her?

"What are you scared of?"

"It's about the open house."

"What about it?"

"I was hoping you'd be there."

"Why?"

"I'm worried. What if they missed something?"

"You mean like maybe something that drained out of Roy and Donny?"

"Don't say it like that."

"How do you want me say it?"

"I knew I shouldn't have called you."

"When's the open house?"

"Sunday, two to four."

Then the phone beeped, alerting me that the call had dropped. Daphne didn't call back and neither did I. We both knew I'd be there.

A CHP cruiser sped past me, lights flashing, and pulled over a car ahead of me. I decided it was time to call it a night. The next one could be me, and I knew there was no way I'd pass a sobriety test. By the time I got home it was too late to do anything except crash. Trouble was, somebody left the lights on, and it wasn't me.

Chapter 10

I sat in the car and looked up at my apartment and wondered who was home instead of me. A shadow moved across the windows that looked out on Valencia Street. Maybe they were enjoying the view. It occurred to me that I should call the police.

But then I thought they'd take one look at me and know I was guilty of something. That was the problem with having something to hide. I decided to go upstairs and introduce myself.

The front door was ajar, as if whoever opened it had a key or knew how to pick a lock. But the only person with a key besides me was the manager, and Cornell wasn't in the habit of stopping by in the middle of the night unless he wanted to spin a few records. I pushed the door open and went inside. The TV was on, tuned to a game. There was a guy sitting on the sofa. He looked to be in his forties, with black curly hair, dark eyes, and a greasy, olive complexion. He wore cargo shorts and a gray fleece vest over a yellow soccer jersey. His hands were in his pockets and his feet were propped up on the coffee table like he lived there.

I stopped cold and stared at him. Froze as my body clenched and I broke out in a sweat. Knock on wood, I'd never been robbed or been on the receiving end of a break-in or a home invasion. And yet here he was, a total stranger, big as life, who'd somehow found his way into my apartment and onto my sofa.

"Who are you? What are doing in my apartment? How'd you get in here?" The questions tumbled through my brain and rushed out of my mouth.

"Too many questions, man," he said with a smile.

He spoke with an accent that sounded Mexican or South American.

"Maybe you should start answering them," I said.

He shrugged, then picked up the remote and turned up the volume on the game. The roar of the crowd thundered through my apartment. I went over to him, grabbed the remote out of his hands and turned off the TV.

"I got neighbors," I said.

He looked up at me and scowled. Then his right hand came out of the vest pocket. I noticed that there was a gun attached to it.

"Sit down," he said, waving the gun at the club chair across from the sofa.

This was the second time somebody had pointed a gun at me, and I didn't like it any more than I did the first time. And I worried that one of these times it might go off.

"You gonna tell me what this is all about?" I said as I sat down.

"You know what it's about."

"I do?"

"Yeah, you do."

"Maybe you should refresh my memory."

"It's about the money. You forget about the money?"

"What money?"

His face tightened and his eyes turned hard as

marbles. He slammed the gun down on the coffee table. "Our money! Me and Tiffany's money!"

Then it hit me. The accent, the money, the girlfriend behind bars who had played dumb about Ronaldo's whereabouts. I wondered what else she was lying about.

"Ronaldo, right?"

"Yeah, straight up, man. So where's the money?"

I scoffed. "What makes you think I know anything about it?"

"Tiffany told me you went to see her."

"Yeah, I went to see her about Vic's obituary."

"She thinks maybe you know where the money is."

I shook my head. It was funny what greed could do to people, especially people whose payday dreams had gone south, along with their freedom.

"She's wrong. I don't know anything about it. So why don't you get out of here before I call the police."

He stood and pushed the gun closer to my face. "You calling my Tiffany a liar?"

I took a deep breath. It was late and I was tired of dealing with people who seemed to think I knew more than I did. When all I did know was that Archie's obit had somehow unleashed a series of events that had snowballed across my life and threatened to bury me. And I wasn't ready to be buried just yet. Enough was enough.

I jumped to my feet and grabbed the gun and pushed it away from me. The move caught Ronaldo by surprise. I could see it in his eyes as he struggled to hold onto the gun. I tightened my grip on it and we wrestled for control. He was strong, stronger than me, but he thought the gun was his, and wasn't prepared to have to fight about it. Then Ronaldo lunged at me, apparently hoping to throw me off balance and force me to let go of the gun. But he forgot about the coffee table. He tripped over it and fell face first onto the hardwood floor. Which I figured had to hurt.

I stood over him with the gun in my hand. He was motionless at first, groaning to himself. Then he rolled over and looked up at me. His forehead was bruised and his nose was smashed, and his face was covered with blood. He looked stunned, as if this wasn't supposed to happen.

"Get out," I said. "And don't come back."

He winced as he slowly pulled himself up, first on one knee, then finally on his own two feet.

"The door's over there," I said, nodding at the front door.

"What about my gun?"

"It's not yours anymore," I said. "It's mine. And if you ever come back here again, I'll use it."

Ronaldo nodded like he got the message, but it was hard to tell, given the dazed look on his face and the fact that his eyes seemed out of focus.

He limped to the door, then turned and looked back at me. "We got it comin', me and Tiffany."

I offered a cold smile. "We all got it coming, Ronaldo."

He turned and staggered out the door. I locked it, then went to the window and watched as he came out of the building onto Valencia Street. He stood on the sidewalk and looked around, as if unsure of his next move, or perhaps even who he was. He looked up at the windows and I wondered if he saw me watching him. I turned off the lights, then raised the gun and took dead aim at Ronaldo. It would have been easy to pick him off.

All I had to do was open the window and pull the trigger. I felt like a sniper as I watched him, and I kept him in my sights until he stumbled off into the dark.

****

I was on my way to Daphne's open house when Nicole called. I thought about letting it go to voicemail. It was too nice a day to talk about murder, but maybe the weather was never right for it.

"Where are you?" she said. "Sounds like you're in the car."

"Yeah, thought I'd take a Sunday drive to a crime scene."

"You're gonna talk to Daphne about it, right?" she said, cutting to the chase.

"Sure, no problem, Nic. I'll just say, 'you've done it twice already, what's one more?'"

"Spare me the sarcasm, okay, Max? We don't have much time. Either Daphne takes him out or we all go down for it."

"Since when did she become the designated hitter?"

"You want to do it?"

"Maybe all three of us could do it, Nic. What do you think of that idea?"

"Seriously, Max? Is this whole thing like some big joke to you?"

"I don't know, Nic, it's like all we talk about now."

"Sorry, I can't stop thinking about it."

"Yeah, I noticed. I don't know about you, but I'm having a hard time wrapping my mind around murder."

"Try wrapping your mind around going to prison. See how that feels."

I said nothing, because just then I rolled off the Richmond-San Rafael Bridge and caught sight of San

Quentin state prison off to the left.

"You hear me?"

"Loud and clear, Nic," I said, as I tried to imagine life behind its walls. But it was impossible. You had to be there. And by then it would be too late. That was the problem.

"What if she agrees to have sex with him?" I said. "Isn't that what he wants?"

"It won't stop there and you know it."

"There's only one way to stop him, right, Nic?"

"You got a better idea?"

Yeah, let's pretend it never happened, I thought.

"I gotta run," Nicole said. "Let me know how it goes."

Then she was gone and suddenly I missed her. Or maybe what I missed was the way it was between us before all this happened. No matter how it all went down, I knew that things would never be the same. I wondered if we could even stay friends, or if the sight of each other would always remind us of what we had done. Pimp her out or put a gun in her hand, Nic said. Then try to walk away like it never happened, I thought.

I looked up at the sky and saw clouds moving in from the coast. When I rolled down the window the air smelled like rain. Would Daphne's open house run with blood if it rained? I had no idea, but her freeway exit was coming up. I moved into the right lane and felt my stomach tighten as the ramp rushed toward me.

The sky had darkened by time I got to Daphne's place, and a sunny day had faded into an overcast afternoon. But that didn't stop the crowd that had parked up and down the street from climbing out of their cars and heading up to the house. I wondered how many of them were there because they wanted a to buy a house, and how many just wanted to cruise a gangster's digs. Archie's pile was a hot property. The funny part was that none of the prospective buyers knew just how hot it was. I hoped for Daphne's sake, and mine, that it stayed that way.

I noticed that the realtor had added an "Open House" sticker to the "For Sale" sign. As I passed the sign, I couldn't help but flash on Donny coming out of the house and making it as far as the sign before he bled out. I realized right then that whenever I saw a realtor's sign, I would also see Donny. I figured that should be enough to keep me out of real estate. As I approached the house, I also noticed that Daphne's convertible was missing from its usual spot in the driveway. I remembered that the last time I saw the car some surfer kid was taking her on what seemed like a joyride through the city. I also remembered that I had followed them, like some jealous boyfriend. I felt my face get hot as I recalled being grateful they weren't holding hands.

The realtor, an Asian woman in jeans and a blazer branded with her company's logo, smiled as I stepped into the house.

"Welcome," she said as she handed me a flier. "Thanks for stopping by. Let me know if you have any questions."

"Thanks," I said with a polite smile. I wasn't sure what to ask at an open house that doubled as a crime scene, and so I moved on.

Buyers clutching fliers were milling around in the living room, chatting and comparing notes. I tried my best to pretend I was one of them. But all I saw was Roy swimming to eternity in a sea of blood, and with all the time in the world to get there. I decided to change the scenery and went outside onto the patio.

Daphne was sitting by the pool. She wore shades that looked good on her and was drinking a glass of lemonade. A pitcher was on the table in front of her. I wondered if it was spiked. She looked up at me and smiled.

"Kim doesn't like me being here, but it's my house, right?" she said. "I can be here if I want."

"Yeah, I guess you can, long as it's yours."

"Won't be mine for much longer."

"Isn't that what you want?"

Daphne shrugged and looked out at the crowd of strangers shuffling through her house.

"Doesn't matter what I want," she said. She took off her shades and looked up at me. "Thanks for coming."

"Sure, no problem." I pulled out a chair and sat next to her. "I didn't see your car in the driveway, wasn't sure if you were here."

"I sold it."

"You sold it?"

Daphne nodded. "Some surfer kid. He's gonna put the top down and put his board in the back."

I smiled, and hoped that would be enough to hide the shame that burned inside me. I had followed her across town because I saw her with another man, and all she was doing was selling her car.

"Want some lemonade?" Daphne said. "We'll have to share the glass. I don't want to go back in the house right now." She reached out and took my hand. I felt the heat of her rush through me. "But we've shared so much already, haven't we?"

Our eyes met and for a moment the open house

faded away and it was just the two of us, sitting outside by the pool. We weren't exactly holding hands, but it was close. And the more I looked at her the more I wanted all of her. Then I remembered that Rikers wanted her too. And I knew that there was still more blood for us to share.

"We have a problem," I said, as the world closed in around us again.

Daphne stiffened. "What are you talking about?"

"Rikers wants his share."

"Share of what? I don't understand."

"He wants to be compensated."

"For what?"

"For the clean-up crew. You remember them, don't you? They made it all go away, like it never happened. Rikers made that happen."

Daphne dismissed the issue with a shrug. "So I'll pay him off once the sale clears. Shouldn't take long."

I paused. Prospective buyers were drifting out into the patio.

"He doesn't want a payoff, Daphne."

"What's he want, then?"

"He wants you."

Daphne's deep brown eyes widened. She stared at me, then laughed out loud. "Me?"

I nodded. "That's the deal."

Daphne scoffed. "That's your deal, Max. Not mine. I didn't make any deals."

"I didn't make a deal, Daphne. I'm just telling you what he wants in return."

"So he wants to fuck me, is that it?"

I looked around to see if anyone had heard her. And if they had, it would probably have been a first at an open house. Then again, this wasn't an ordinary open house.

"Yeah, that's what he wants."

"And you're supposed to pimp me out, right?"

I felt my face get hot. "You think I like this? You think I like any part of this? You gunned down two people, Daphne. If you're lucky, you'll get away with it. But if he doesn't get what he wants you won't."

Her eyes froze with alarm. "What do you mean?"

"He's a CI, a confidential informant. He'll go to the cop he snitches for and hang us all out to dry."

Daphne paused, then said, "I see." She took a sip of lemonade. "You want some?"

I shook my head. "I'm good."

She looked out at the buyers prowling around the patio. "It's a good crowd, don't you think? Maybe we'll get some offers."

"Look, Daphne, about Rikers, you don't have to do this—"

She turned to me and I saw that her eyes had gone cold. "You know what, Max? Maybe I should just shoot him."

My breath caught in my throat. "Jesus, Daphne. You can't just go around shooting people."

"I don't like people telling me I have to fuck them. What if I don't want to fuck him? What then? And what if once isn't enough?"

I said nothing. She was starting to sound a lot like Nicole and it scared me. The whole damn thing scared me. And yet when I looked at her I knew I could never walk away, and that really scared me.

"Maybe you just meet him," I said. "See how it goes."

"You mean see if I want screw him or shoot him?"

I took a deep breath and let it out slowly. "Yeah, something like that."

Daphne smiled. "Remember when you asked me if I still had the gun?"

I nodded. "Yeah, I remember. You told me you might need to use it again."

"And here we are."

"Yeah, here we are," I said, "and I wish to hell we weren't."

Daphne smiled. "You worry too much, baby. It'll all work out, one way or the other."

Screw him or shoot him, the lady said, and I wasn't sure which she liked better. I looked around and noticed that the buyers who had been checking out the patio had gone back inside. The sliding doors were still open, and I could see that people were leaving. I checked my watch and saw it was almost four. Soon it would be just the two of us.

Just then the realtor stepped out onto the patio and came up to the table. She gave me a curious look, as if I was supposed to be gone by now, and said, "You're still here?"

"He's a friend," Daphne said. She looked up at Kim. "So how'd it go?"

"Great. Got lots of interest. We'll do another one next weekend and then we can review offers."

Daphne shook her head. "I don't want to do another one, Kim."

"You don't?" Kim said, a surprised expression on her face. "We'll get more offers, you know."

"I think one's enough. Let's see what today brings, okay?"

"Sure, whatever you say, Daphne. I'll let you

know." Kim reached into her purse. "By the way, look what I found." She pulled out a fake hundred-dollar bill and handed it to Daphne. "Looks real, doesn't it?"

"Where'd you find it?" Daphne said, looking at the bill.

"It was on the floor in the office. Funny, huh?"

"Yeah, funny," Daphne said.

I flashed on Vic's order of play money and wondered if it was part of the same stash. And if it was, what was it doing in Archie's house?

"Don't spend it all in one place," Kim said with a smile. "And let me know if you change your mind about another open house." Then she turned and walked away.

"She's not too happy with me," Daphne said. "I guess I'm not greedy enough."

"Maybe you're just desperate," I said.

She turned to me. "Yeah, maybe I am. Can't blame a girl for being desperate, can you?" Then she crumpled the hundred-dollar bill in her hand.

"Hi," I heard a man say.

Daphne heard him too. We both looked up and saw a young couple in their twenties standing by the sliding doors. They wore shabby thrift shop clothing and looked like the homeless kids you saw panhandling on Haight Street, pretending that the sixties never ended. I noticed the woman was pregnant.

Daphne and I exchanged puzzled glances.

"Sorry," the woman said, "the front door was open."

"Can I help you?" Daphne said. "The open house is over."

"We're not here about the open house," the man said.

"We heard the gunshots," the woman said with a sly smile. "We saw what happened."

Chapter 11

Daphne froze, stared at her uninvited guests as though she was hallucinating. I figured the shocked expression on her face matched my own. She was gripping her glass of lemonade so tightly that her knuckles were turning white. I imagined the glass shattering and then having to rush her to the nearest ER, the two of us covered in blood. Then again, we were already covered in blood. I didn't know much about open houses, but this had to be one for the books.

Who could have seen it, I wondered. Who was around to hear two gunshots in the dark in the middle of the night? They were around, that's who. It was always the thing you least expected that could really hang you up. And in this case, the thing we least expected was a pair of junior panhandlers from the Haight. Go figure. But what were they doing in the hills so far from home?

"Excuse me? What did you say?" Daphne said, still trying to process what had happened, the shock wearing off so that now she was just stunned.

"Nice place you got here," the man said, ignoring Daphne's question. He looked around the patio as the two of them sauntered over to us. "How come you're selling it?"

"I don't think that's any of your business," Daphne said.

"Guess not," the man said with shrug, "just asking."

"Sorry, Mick gets kinda nosy," the woman said.

"Shut up, Janis," the man said.

Were those really their names, I wondered, or were they both so deep into their sixties trip that they'd borrowed the names of rock stars?

"You mind if I sit down?" Janis said, her hands on her belly.

"Sure, make yourself at home," Daphne said.

"Thanks," Janis said as she pulled out a chair and sat down. "We walked all the way over here."

Walked all the way over from where, I wondered. Haight Street?

"You walked over here?" I said.

Mick nodded. "We're hanging out in the house down the road."

Then it hit me. I thought I'd seen someone on the upper deck when I passed the house on my way to Daphne's to interview her for Archie's obit, and now I knew it wasn't my imagination. It was real. Dead real.

"You mean the house that's under construction?"

Janis nodded. "Yeah, we just kinda found the place and decided to hang out for a while."

"We wanted to get out of the city, what with the baby coming and all," Mick said.

"The weather's so nice here," Janis said. "Kinda what we were looking for."

"What are you gonna do when they start working on the house again?" I said.

Mick shrugged. "I guess we'll move on. We figured you could help us out with that."

"Is that why you're here?" Daphne said.

"Like we said, we saw what happened."

"We came right away when we heard the shots,"

Janis said.

"It was cool how they cleaned it all up and got rid of the bodies."

"We laughed when we saw what it said on the side of the van."

"Like it never happened, right?"

"So why didn't you go to the police?" I said.

"Cops ain't gonna do nothin' for us," Mick said.

"But we are, right?" Daphne said. "We're gonna do something for you."

"We just want what's fair," Janis said.

"What's fair?" Daphne said.

Mick shrugged. "You tell me. We saw the house was for sale and figured there was something in it for us. We just want everybody to be happy, you know."

"Yeah, I know," Daphne said. "Would you excuse me? I'll be right back."

"Sure, no problem."

Daphne stood and walked toward the sliding doors. A feeling of dread came over me as I watched her disappear into the house. Or was it that she scared me no matter what she did?

"You guys married?" Janis said. She glanced at Mick. "Me and Mick, we're gonna get married soon as the baby comes."

I looked up at her. She was smiling at me, like we were about to have a conversation about kids and home and family, the whole shebang. But they hadn't stopped by for small talk or a glass of lemonade.

"Cut the crap, both of you," I said. "How much do you want?"

Mick and Janis exchanged startled glances. Money was why they were here. They just didn't know how to talk about it.

"Whatever, you know," Mick said, fumbling for words.

"No, I don't know. How much?"

"A hundred grand?" Janis said.

"To keep your mouth shut, right?"

Mick and Janis traded glances again, then Mick said, "Well, yeah…"

"And how we know you're gonna do that?"'

"Do what?"

"Keep your mouth shut."

"Hey, we're not gonna tell nobody…you pay us, we're gone, man—"

"Like it never happened, right?" I said.

Mick smiled like we'd just made a deal. "You got it."

Just then Daphne walked back out onto the patio. A purse was slung over her shoulder. I wondered if she was going to pull out her checkbook and write the expectant couple a check. She came up the table and opened the purse. Then she pulled out the gun she used to clip Roy and Donny and pointed it at Mick and Janis.

We all stared at the gun. Three people sitting by the pool and staring down the barrel of a 9mm Glock. As if it had come out of nowhere. But I knew better. I could hear Janis whimpering as the fear overtook her. Mick, on the other hand, was sucking air like he was afraid it would run out. Me, I was just hoping I was still on Daphne's good side.

She stood by the table at point-blank range, and the look in her eyes was enough to scare anybody. The gun made it worse.

"Daphne…" I said, as calmly as possible under the

circumstances.

"What?" she snapped, her eyes on Mick and Janis.

"Put the gun down, okay?"

"I can't yet."

"Why not?"

"I haven't decided whether to shoot them or not."

Did she mean what she said, I wondered. Or was she just trying to scare them? She could've saved herself the trouble. They were freaked the minute the gun came out of her purse. Had she given herself a moment to decide whether to shoot Roy and Donny? Somehow I doubted it.

"Please don't shoot my baby..." Janis wailed.

"I'm not gonna shoot your baby, *Janis,*" Daphne said. "But I might shoot you."

"Just let us go, we won't say nothin'," Mick said.

Daphne scoffed. "Right. Next you're gonna tell me you forgot all about it."

Janis glared at Mick, her eyes flashing with accusation. "I told you this wasn't gonna work."

"Shut the fuck up!" Mick said.

"Did you really think you were gonna get away with it?" Daphne said. "Seriously?"

Mick and Janis exchanged glances. If they had an answer to Daphne's question, they kept it to themselves. I imagined them rushing to the house when they heard the shots, then hiding in the dark and watching Ernie and Janelle clean up the crime scene. It probably seemed like a good idea at the time to try and cash in on what they saw. Instead, they found themselves on the wrong end of a gun.

"How much do they want?" Daphne said.

"A hundred grand."

Robert Baty

"For the baby, right?" she said with a scornful smile.

"I never had a baby before," Janis said, starting to cry. "I don't know what to do. We don't have any money, don't have a place to live…we just thought—"

"You saw what happened and thought this could work, right?"

Janis hung her head. Her cheeks were streaked with tears. Mick reached over and tried to take her hand, but she pulled away from him.

"I think they got the message, Daphne. You can put the gun down now," I said.

But Daphne kept the gun pointed at Mick and Janis. I got the feeling she liked what she was doing. Liked the gun in her hand and liked pointing it at people.

"Why? So they can turn us in?"

Mick shook his head. "No way, you gotta believe me, we're not gonna tell anybody."

"There's only one way to make sure."

Janis's wailing got louder. She was starting to sound like a siren, which somehow seemed appropriate under the circumstances. I had to admit that I had no idea what Daphne would do next, but adding to the body count was the last thing we needed. I scraped back my chair and stood.

"Enough, okay?" I nodded at the gun. "Put it down."

Daphne looked sharply at me, as if surprised that I would challenge her. Her grip on the gun seemed to tighten.

"What if I have to shoot them?"

"You're not shooting anybody," I said. At least not today, I thought.

"We can't just let them go, Max…they saw what happened."

"We didn't see nothin'!" Mick said.

"Shut up!" Daphne said, glaring at Mick. "You saw what happened and that's why you're here." She turned to me. "We have to do something, don't you see?"

"We don't have to shoot them, Daphne."

Daphne paused to consider it, then said, "You got a better idea?"

"Yeah, I do," I said, "but first you've got to put the gun down."

Daphne glanced at me and smiled.

"Why should I?"

"Because we don't want it to go off, okay?"

She was still smiling when I reached over and grabbed the gun out of her hands and put it on the table. Daphne stared at me, stunned that I had disarmed her. I had to admit I was a bit stunned myself. I knew she could easily pick it up again, but at least for the moment her finger wasn't on the trigger.

I didn't have a better idea, unless keeping them alive was better than shooting them and then trying to figure out how to dispose of two more bodies. And who would clean up the mess this time around? We were already in hock to Rikers for Ernie and Janelle.

Daphne gave herself a moment to think about it, then sat down and poured herself a glass of lemonade.

She took a sip, then looked at me and said, "I'm listening."

"We give 'em what they want," I said.

Mick and Janis exchanged surprised glances. Daphne's eyes narrowed with suspicion.

"Excuse me?"

"A hundred grand."

"I don't have a hundred grand, Max. I don't have a

dime until the house sells and you know it."

"We can wait," Mick said.

Daphne gave a cold smile. "I'll bet you can."

"No rush, you know, we're easy," Janis said.

"What about your car?" I said.

Daphne looked at me. "What about it? I sold it."

"Give 'em what you got for it, and pay 'em the rest when the house clears."

"Just like that, huh?"

"Yeah, just like that." I glanced at Mick and Janis. "You good with that?"

Mick nodded. "Yeah, sure we are." He exchanged glances with Janis, who looked relieved, then nodded at the gun. "But how do we know she's not gonna shoot us?"

"You don't," Daphne said.

Mick scowled. "What the fuck's that supposed to mean?"

"It means I'm a woman," Daphne said with a teasing smile. "We change our minds all the time." She glanced at Janis. "Isn't that right, Janis?"

"Nobody's gonna shoot anybody," I said. "But if you talk, you're dead."

"What we gonna talk about?" Mick said. "We didn't see nothin'."

"I hope not, for your sake." I glanced at Daphne. "Do we have a deal?"

Daphne shrugged but said nothing. I searched her face for an answer, but all I saw was a mask. It was beautiful, but it was still a mask. Then she smiled, and suddenly I got worried.

"That's a good idea, Max," she said. "But I have a better idea."

"Yeah? What's that?" I said, as my stomach tightened into a knot.

"They kill Rikers, then they get their hundred grand."

The punch I never saw coming nearly knocked me out of my chair. I stared, dumbfounded, at the woman sitting across the table from me.

Mick and Janis exchanged puzzled glances, then Mick said, "Who's Rikers?"

My cellphone rang. I stepped away from the table to take the call.

"It's me," Nicole said.

"Hey, what's up?"

"You talk to her?"

"Yeah, I talked to her."

"And?"

"I'll tell you later."

"No, tell me now."

"I can't."

"Why not?"

I glanced at Daphne. "Because you won't believe it."

Two beeps later the call dropped and Nicole was gone. It was just as well. I remembered what Daphne had told me about sketchy cell reception in the hills, and for once I was grateful to lose a call. The last thing I wanted to do was have to explain why Daphne wouldn't be screwing or shooting Rikers. Instead, she'd decided to outsource the hit to a homeless, panhandling couple from the Haight. I knew I'd have to come clean sooner or later, but would it really matter when we talked about it, or who pulled the trigger? The blood would still be on our hands. I stood with my back to the table and looked out at the pool, and suddenly felt as if I was underwater and never coming up for air.

Then I heard Janis say in a raised voice this side of soprano, "You want us to kill somebody?"

I turned and looked at the happy trio sitting around the table.

"You want the money, don't you?" Daphne said.

"Yeah, we want the money," Mick said. "But why us? We don't know nothin' about killing people."

There's nothing to it, I thought, flashing on Roy and Donny. Just point and shoot.

"The money doesn't come free, Mick," Daphne said. "You need to do something for me in return."

"We are doing something for you—we're keeping our mouths shut about what we saw."

"That's not enough."

"What if we talk? You're gonna be in deep shit then, aren't you?"

"I wouldn't, if I were you," I said. "You've got a kid on the way, he's gonna need a father."

Mick looked up at me and I could see the fear and confusion in his eyes. "You threatening me?"

I said nothing, just stared him down until he looked away. I was threatening him. I'd never threatened anybody, and yet here I was threatening an expectant father. The thought of it filled me with shame. Daphne looked at me and smiled, as if to say she approved of my tactics, and that made me feel even worse. But I was in too deep to stop, and she knew it.

"I'm not killing anybody!" Janis said, holding her belly as she started to get up from her chair.

"Sit down!" Mick said, pulling her back down into the chair.

"Let go of me!" Janis said.

"Listen to me," Mick said, looking up at Janis. "Just sit down and listen to me, okay?"

Janis sighed, then sat down again.

"We need the money, babe," Mick said. "What are we gonna do with a baby and no money and no place to live?"

I felt embarrassed, like I was some kind of voyeur, watching them as they came around to the idea of murder for the good of the family. I wondered if Daphne felt the same way, or if she was somehow getting off on it.

"Who is Rikers anyway?" Janis said.

"He's a problem," Daphne said.

"What kind of problem?"

Daphne smiled. "The kind that won't go away..."

"Unless he's dead, right?"

Daphne slid the gun across the table to Mick. "You could do a lot with a hundred thousand cash, Mick."

Janis drew back at the sight of the gun, but Mick leaned in to it.

"Go ahead," Daphne said, "pick it up, see how it feels."

Mick smiled, like a kid who'd suddenly been given permission, then picked up the gun.

"Mick, please, I don't want to do this..." Janis said, with a look in her eyes that said nothing good would come of this.

"It's heavy," Mick said, feeling the weight of the gun in his hand.

"You get used to it," Daphne said. Then, as if it had just occurred to her, she picked up the empty pitcher of lemonade and held it out to me. "Max, since you're up, would you mind? There's more in the fridge."

"Sure, no problem," I said.

I took the pitcher and went into the house. For a minute I thought about skipping the lemonade and heading straight out the door to my car and what was left of my life. Then again, that would have been too easy. Daphne would be waiting for me wherever I was, along with everybody else who'd showed up ever since I filed Archie's obit. I went into the kitchen and refilled the pitcher of lemonade. Then I set it on the counter and stood by the window and looked out at the patio. Mick still had the gun in his hands, and looked as though he was warming up to the idea of using it. All he needed now was for Nicole and me to push Rikers into the line of fire.

I picked up the pitcher and was about to go back outside when something caught my eye. It was on the floor, in the narrow space between the fridge and the stove. I bent down and picked it up, and saw that it was a woody station wagon fridge magnet. The words "Woody Wonders" appeared below the image of the car. I smiled at the sight of it. I'd always loved woodies, but what was Daphne doing with it? Was she into woodies or vintage cars? Somehow she didn't seem the type. Or was it Archie? I thought of my muscle car ride parked in the driveway and wondered if we had more in common than I knew.

I pictured Daphne's fridge covered with magnets, maybe pics of her and Archie in happier times. A gangster in love with his femme fatale. I figured her realtor had instructed her to take them down for the open house, and Daphne hadn't noticed that the woody had fallen on the floor. She wouldn't miss it, I thought, and slipped it into my pocket. Why did I take it? I wasn't sure, exactly. I just wanted it. Maybe because I'd always thought it would be fun to have a woody. Or maybe because I wanted to know more about what "Woody Wonders" had to do with Archie Gibbs. I was about to rejoin the party when my phone rang.

"We've got a problem," Nicole said.

Then another voice came on the line.

"She means me," Rikers said.

Chapter 12

I called Daphne from the car. "The lemonade's on the counter."

"What?" she said, sounding confused. "What do you mean, it's on counter? Where are you?"

"Something came up."

"You left?"

"Yeah, I left."

"Without saying goodbye?"

I said nothing. I heard footsteps, and figured she'd stepped away from the table.

"I need you, Max."

I let it sink in. It went in deep. I wanted her to need me, even though it scared me. And I guess I needed her too for all the wrong reasons.

"I'll call you later. Are they still there?"

"Yes, of course they are. I thought you'd still be here too."

"So did I."

"So what's so important you had to rush off without saying goodbye?"

"It's about Rikers."

"What about him?"

"I don't know yet. Some kind of problem. That's all I know."

"We need to take him out, don't we?"

"You think they're up for it?"

"Mick and Janis?"

"Yeah."

"I think they're getting used to the idea."

How do you get used to the idea of murder, I wondered. Spend enough time around Daphne Swan and you get used to anything.

"So when am I gonna hear from you?" she said.

"Later. Soon as I know more."

"Don't forget about me, Max. Not after all we've been through."

Fat chance of that, I thought as she ended the call.

An hour later, I corkscrewed to the top level of a rundown parking garage for an abandoned mall in South City. The mall had shut down but the garage was still standing. Only now instead of bustling with cars and customers on a Sunday afternoon it was filled with garbage, graffiti, and homeless. It was called the Sunrise Mall, but the fact was the sun had set on the place years ago. I figured Rikers picked it because he wanted to make sure we met where no one that mattered would see him. Then again, I thought, maybe he liked the vibe.

Nicole was already there, waiting in her SUV. I rolled up next to her and killed the engine. She looked over at me, then got out of the car. She walked around the car, then climbed in on the passenger side and pulled the door shut.

"So what's the problem?" I said.

"He wouldn't tell me. Said he'd tell us when we got together."

"So where is he?"

Nic looked sharply at me. "Like I'm supposed to know?"

"Hey, take it easy, Nic. I don't like this any more

than you do."

"Sorry, this place gives me the creeps," she said. She looked around the crumbling structure, then turned to me. "You said on the phone I wouldn't believe you."

I nodded.

"Try me," she said.

I looked up at her we locked eyes.

"Is it about Daphne?"

"Yeah."

"You said you talked to her, right?"

"Yeah, I did."

"So what happened?"

I took a deep breath, then braced her on Mick and Janis and what they'd seen, and how Daphne had decided they should clip Rikers in return for a generous contribution to the family fund.

"Seriously?" Nicole said, eyes wide. "A couple of hippies from the Haight?"

I nodded.

"Why?"

"I think she's getting off on it."

"What do they know about shooting somebody?"

"About as much as we know."

"They'll screw it up, Max." She paused. "Then we'll have to do it."

Just then, a black muscle car rumbled onto the level. I looked over at the car.

"Is that him?"

"Yeah, that's him."

I could hear the thump of hip hop getting louder as the car approached. Rikers pulled up next to me on the driver's side and looked out at us. I could see he was eating a cheeseburger. Then he lowered the window and an angry rap punched its way out of the car. Rikers sat behind the wheel, his head nodding to the beat. Then he turned off the music and for a moment the only thing I heard was him chewing with his mouth open.

"Glad you guys could make it," he said.

"Did we have a choice?" I said.

Rikers shrugged his shoulders and took a bite of his burger.

"Not really."

"You said we had a problem."

Rikers nodded at his back seat. "Have a seat."

I heard a click as he unlocked the doors. Nic and I exchanged glances.

"I don't like this," Nic said.

"Which part?"

We climbed out of our cars and joined Rikers. The car smelled like fast food grease and stale beer. Rikers glanced at us in the rearview.

"So what's the problem?" I said.

"Ernie and Janelle."

"What about them?"

"They got busted for speeding and the cops found guns in the car," Rikers said, eating his burger. "We gotta get rid of 'em."

Nic and I exchanged glances.

"The guns?" Nic said.

Rikers shook his head. "Ernie and Janelle."

Nic stared at Rikers, then opened the door. "I'm out of here," she said, and climbed out of the car.

"Nic! Wait!" I said, jumping out of the car.

She headed to her SUV and was about to open the door and slide in behind the wheel when I caught up to her and grabbed her arm.

"Nic, will you wait a minute?"

"Let go of me!" she said, shaking loose of me.

I put up my hands in complete surrender. "Can we talk, okay?"

"Talk?" Nic, said, her eyes flashing with anger. "What do you want to talk about, Max? How we're gonna get rid of Ernie and Janelle? You started this mess; you figure it out." She turned away from me and opened the door.

"It's not that simple, Knickers," I heard Rikers say.

Nicole let the door hang open and we both looked over at Rikers. He was leaning against his car with a sneering know-it-all smile on his face that made me want to punch him in the mouth.

"If they talk, we all go down."

"What are they gonna talk about?" I said. "They got busted for guns, not bodies, right?"

"Might start out talking about guns, but they might end up talking about bodies. Especially if those bodies happen to turn up. You want to take that chance?"

I felt my head start to spin and wondered if Nicole felt the same way. We were planning a hit on Ernie and Janelle with the same guy that we planned to hit. In fact, Daphne already had a couple of first timers all lined up. Did Rikers have a clue that he was a target? I had no idea, but the whole thing was making me dizzy. And what about us, me and Nicole? We were running out of people to shoot. When was our number coming up? When were the guns going to be turned on us?

Nicole sighed. She looked around the parking garage as though she was searching for a place to hide.

"You said they got arrested," she said.

Rikers nodded.

"So how are you going get to them if they're in jail?"

I glanced at her. She knew she was in a nightmare that was snowballing into an even worse nightmare, but she was still thinking it through. I figured that was what made her a good reporter. She followed the story to its logical conclusion, even when it led to a dead end.

"We bail 'em out," Rikers said.

Nicole stared at him. "What, so we can kill them once they're out?"

"Works for me," Rikers said.

"I can't believe this," Nicole said. "So why don't you do it? You're the one who wants to get rid of them."

"That's not the deal," Rikers said.

"Excuse me? The deal was Daphne, Rikers. Not murder."

"Still is. I just added something a little extra."

"Why not bail 'em out and then help 'em jump bail?" I said.

"We can't be sure," Rikers said. "What if they get caught? You think they're not gonna roll over?"

"I don't know…" Nic said. "I have to think about this."

"No problem," Rikers said. "But think fast. We don't have much time. I'll be in touch."

Rikers got back in his car. The engine rumbled to life. Then he lowered the window and the music thundered across the parking garage like it was looking for a fight. Nic and I watched as he spun the car around the pavement like he was showing off, then headed back down the ramp. The sounds faded into silence, and we looked at each other and thought of something to say.

"This isn't happening, is it, Max?"

I said nothing. It was happening, and we both knew

it.

"I'm sorry I got you mixed up in it, Nic."

"Too late for that now, Max. You should be sorry you got yourself mixed up in it."

"Trust me, I am."

"Really?" Nicole said, a skeptical look on her face. "Are you sorry about her too?"

I met her gaze, then looked away.

"She has her hooks in you, doesn't she? How's it feel?"

"How do you think it feels?" I said sharply, feeling the heat rush into my face.

"What about that couple?"

I looked up at her. "You mean Mick and Janis?"

Nic offered a scornful smile. "Mick and Janis? Seriously?"

I nodded.

"If they take Rikers out we're off the hook, right?"

"That's a big if, Nic."

"What if we have to do it?"

I looked at her and saw that something had gone dead in her eyes, and I hated seeing it.

"Let's take it one step at a time, okay, Nic? Maybe they'll get lucky."

"So what's the next step?"

"I hate to admit it, but Rikers is right about one thing. We need to bail 'em out before they cop a plea."

"Just like that, huh? You know how much that's gonna cost?"

"You're the crime reporter, Nic. You tell me."

"Do the math, Max. Ballpark, could be anywhere from fifty, sixty grand each. Maybe more if they're repeat offenders. Ten percent of that is ten to twelve thousand. You got the cash for that? Because I sure don't."

"No, but I've got an idea."

Chapter 13

I had an idea, I told her. What a joke. Did Nicole even believe me? Did I believe myself, I wondered, as I headed north on 101 back to the city. I ran out of ideas the day I met Daphne Swan. Now I was driving fast on a one-way trip to hell, because the sooner you got there the better the devil liked it.

But this wasn't just about me. I'd dragged Nic into it too, maybe because I didn't know what else to do, and now she was along for the ride. She didn't deserve it, and I figured the least I could do was try and make sure she didn't go down with the rest of us. And right now that meant getting Ernie and Janelle out of jail before they talked themselves into a deal and before Roy and Donny spoiled the party by turning up dead in a dumpster or a landfill.

But that wasn't the only reason I wanted to get them out. I guess maybe I wanted to save them too. They'd done Daphne and me a favor and didn't deserve to die for it. I wanted to save everybody except myself, maybe because I didn't know how to save myself. Or maybe I didn't mind as long as Daphne was there too. Get them out so we could execute them, that was Rikers' bright idea. You had to admire the logic. The man definitely knew how to think his way through a problem. You can't shoot them while they're in jail, so bail them out and then shoot them. Give them a taste of freedom before the lights go out.

It made perfect sense on some level. The only problem was that Nic and I were never going to pull the trigger, and maybe Rikers knew that all along. Maybe he was just using us to get them out so he could shoot them. Or maybe he just wanted to see how far he could push us because he got off on it. I didn't much like getting pushed, especially by a snitch, and figured that maybe it was time to push back if we were ever going to make it out alive. I didn't have the cash or the credit card balance to bail them out, and I knew Nic didn't either. But I figured the legend of Archie's last big score was enough to motivate folks to do all sorts of things they hadn't planned on doing, even when they were footing the bill. But if I was wrong, and greed wasn't enough, Ernie and Janelle were going nowhere fast.

These thoughts tumbled through my mind in no particular order as I pulled up in front of Scot Free Bail Bonds. It was a Sunday afternoon, but I knew they'd be open. Crime never took the weekend off, and neither did bail bondsmen.

I stepped to the door and went inside. The waiting room was filled with what I assumed were the friends and family of the incarcerated. They sat patiently staring into their hands, waiting for the opportunity to cough up ten percent. A skinny brunette wearing glasses on a lanyard sat at a desk, her face buried in what I assumed were bail applications.

Ida, the queen of reception, was holding court from behind the front desk, just like last time. She wore a leopard skin top and matching ankle boots, and looked surprised to see me. To tell you the truth, I was surprised to find myself there. She smiled, as if she was expecting good news, and it was then that I thought things might work out after all.

"Bailing somebody out?" she said.

Just me, I thought. Ida picked up the phone and punched in a number. "He's back," she said. Then she put down the phone and leaned in close, and as I inhaled the scent of her perfume I could've sworn I heard the beat of jungle drums. "You get the bitch to come clean?"

My eyes darted around the room. I wondered if anyone had heard her. The skinny brunette never looked up and neither did anyone else. I realized that it probably didn't matter much to this crowd whether they heard her or not. They weren't here for Sunday services.

Then a door opened, and Benny stepped out of his office. He had his hands on his hips and a smile on his face, like he was sizing me up. Ida looked over at him. They exchanged glances, then Ida turned to the skinny brunette and said, "Terri?"

Terri looked up from her paperwork and Ida cocked her head toward the back office. Terri nodded like she didn't care one way or another and went back to work.

"We'll talk in the office," Ida said.

"Great," I said, trying to sound as though I believed it.

Ida stood and I followed her across the room toward the office. As I approached Benny, it struck me that there was something weird about his face. Then I realized that he was wearing makeup.

"Good to see you again," he said as we stepped into the office, and he closed the door behind me.

I looked around the office and saw that it had been set up for a photo shoot. There were umbrella lights on stands and a camera mounted on a tripod, and one wall was draped with white seamless paper. A photographer dressed in black and rocking a black ponytail was fiddling with the camera. Was Benny having his portrait taken, I wondered. Was that why he wore makeup? Or did he just like wearing it?

A stocky, solidly built white guy who looked as if he'd just stepped out of the ring was there too, sitting in one of the chairs across from Benny's desk. He was in his thirties, with short, choppy hair, and he wore a Scot Free Bail Bonds T-shirt and sweatpants.

"We're ready, Mr. Velasco," the photographer said, looking up from his camera.

"Great," Benny said. He turned to me. "I'll be with you a minute."

"Sure, no problem," I said.

Benny nodded at the guy in the Scot Free Bail Bonds T-shirt. "Showtime, Howard."

Howard jumped to his feet like he'd just he'd just heard the bell ring for round one.

"You ready?" Benny said.

"Born ready, Mr. Velasco."

The photographer posed them in front of the seamless backdrop, then stepped back behind the camera. Ida arranged herself on the love seat and watched the proceedings with an expectant look on her face.

"Big smiles as you shake hands, guys," the photographer said as he studied the image on the camera's LCD display.

Benny and Howard exchanged glances, then smiled and shook hands as they stared at the camera. Benny towered over Howard, which made them look like some kind of odd couple. I wondered what the point was and why Benny was posing with the guy. Then I realized that Benny was probably shooting a new addition to the wall of portraits showing him with happy inmates he'd sprung from jail. The shutter fired repeatedly as the photographer took a series of pics. Then he stopped and looked up from the camera.

"We good?" Benny said.

The photographer nodded. "I'll send you the pics and you can decide which one you like," he said, and started unscrewing the camera from the tripod. "Once we're done, I'll come back for the rest of the gear."

"Sounds good," Benny said. "But leave the camera." He threw a teasing smile at Ida. "I might want to take some pinup shots of Ida."

Ida smiled seductively, and I wondered if she'd ever been a stripper.

"You're gonna get him all excited, hon," she said, nodding at the photographer.

The photographer managed a weak smile and stepped back from the camera. I got the feeling that leaving it behind was the last thing he wanted to do. Howard, on the other hand, looked like he couldn't wait to get started.

"Sure, no problem, whatever you need," the photographer said, and stepped to the door. When he got there he looked back at the camera as if he was never going to see it again, then walked out of the office.

Benny turned to Howard. "You got time to stick around?"

"Got all day, Mr. Velasco," he said, as he waited for the party to get started.

Benny smiled and clapped him on the shoulder. He nodded at a chair. "Take a load off."

Howard nodded and sat down.

Ida cocked her head in my direction. "Find out what he wants, hon."

Benny glanced at her. "Workin' on it right now, pumpkin." Then he turned to me. "So, what are you doing here? You got something for us?"

"Just wanted to let you know that I'm getting close."

Benny and Ida exchanged glances.

"Getting close," Ida said. "What the fuck does that mean?"

As if on cue, Howard scowled at me. I wondered if that was why Benny wanted him to stay.

"I picked up a clue from Daphne and got a lead on the goods," I said, tap-dancing as fast as I could.

"What's the lead?" Benny said.

"Looks like he stashed the goods in a storage locker somewhere…just got to get her to tell me where." It sounded lame even to me.

Benny's face tightened. "That's it?"

"Told you the bitch was holding out on us," Ida chimed in.

"That's all you got?" Benny said.

"Just wanted to keep you posted," I said.

"Just wanted to keep us posted, huh? We don't need you to keep us posted; we need you to find it."

Benny nodded at Howard, who stepped forward and punched me in the stomach.

The blow nearly knocked me off my feet. I gasped and doubled up as I clutched what was left of my stomach. Now I knew why Benny had asked him to stick around.

"You follow?" Benny said as he helpfully guided me into a chair.

"Yeah, I got it. But here's the thing—"

"What thing?" Ida said.

"I need your help with something," I gasped, struggling to get the words out, "or we're never gonna find it."

Out of the corner of my eye I saw Howard winding up to throw another punch. But Benny raised his arm to stop him. Howard nodded, a crestfallen look on his face, then sat down across from me and cracked his knuckles.

"What kind of help?" Ida said in a suspicious tone of voice.

I looked up at Ida. "I need you to bail two people out of jail before they cop a plea."

I knew it didn't make sense—it barely made sense to me. I hoped I'd have a chance to explain before Howard took another swing at me. But Benny and Ida looked puzzled, and that worried me. The whereabouts of Archie's score was already a puzzle. They didn't need another one.

Benny shook his head wearily, as if he was disappointed in me. "We gotta bail somebody out?"

"What the hell's that gotta do with Archie's score?" Ida said. She looked at Benny. "Hon, this boy ain't makin' sense."

"No shit," Benny said. His face crumpled with disgust. He nodded at Howard. "Hit him again."

"Sure, no problem, Mr. Velasco," Howard said. He stood and clenched his fists, then moved in for the kill.

"Wait a minute, please!" I said. My eyes darted from Benny to Howard and back again. "I can explain!"

Benny raised his hand again, and Howard stood down. He slumped in a chair and glared at me. He wanted a punching bag, and I was the next best thing.

"Go ahead, explain," he said. "But you better start making sense fast."

"How come we gotta bail 'em out, and what's that got to do with Archie's score?" Ida said.

"Everything," I said. "If they talk, Daphne goes down, and if she goes down, I go down with her." I paused to let it sink in. "If that happens, you're never gonna see a dime of the money."

Benny and Ida exchanged glances again, then Benny walked over to his desk and sat down.

"Who the fuck are they?" he said.

A crime scene cleanup crew, I thought to myself. But that wasn't the answer. Not a good one, anyway. My mind raced with the whirlwind my life had become since the day I interviewed Daphne for Archie's obit. Where would I even begin to tell such an improbable story? How would I describe the events that careened through my brain in a way that only made sense if you were there? I was there, and I still found it hard to believe. But time was running out, and I knew that Benny and Ida were short on patience. And so, before Howard had a chance to step back into the ring, I let the story spill out of me and hoped I could get to the end before Howard landed another punch.

I braced Benny and Ida on everything that happened, from the day I met Daphne, to Roy and Donny, to Rikers, to Ernie and Janelle, and the hippies from the Haight with a gun in their hands. The only thing I left out was the lemonade. The deeper I got into it the more it sounded like a movie I'd like to see, if only it wasn't real. I could tell that Benny and Ida were on the edge of their seats as the tale went on. Even Howard was all ears.

When I got to the end I stopped talking and the room

fell silent. The muffled sounds of conversation bled through the walls from the waiting room. Then Ida laughed out loud.

"You got yourself into some deep shit, didn't you, boy?"

I looked up at her and said nothing. The story spoke for itself.

"And now you want us to get you out of it, right?" Benny said. "Is that about the size of it? I got that right?"

"You want the money, don't you? If Ernie and Janelle cop a plea we're done."

"No, you're done."

"What about the money?"

"Who says we need you to find it?"

"You got a better idea? Isn't that why you called me in the first place?" I said, glancing at Ida. "Because you figured I could get Daphne to tell me where Archie stashed it. Or maybe where she stashed it?"

"Where she stashed it is more like it," Ida said.

"I think you're right, Ida," I said, playing along. "You think she's gonna talk if she goes down for murder?"

Benny and Ida exchanged glances. I could see the flicker of doubt in their eyes, and figured it was the only thing standing between me and Howard's fists.

"He's got a point, hon."

"So we bail these mooks out, then what?" Benny said.

"We help 'em jump bail."

Wrong answer, I thought, soon as I said it. But it was as though I needed to blurt out the truth, even if it was a mistake. I wanted to save Ernie and Janelle, but at the moment I was having trouble saving myself. Out of the corner of my eye I caught a flicker of nod from Benny. It wasn't much, but it was enough to send Howard back into the ring. He delivered a powerful right hook that knocked me out of my chair and sent me skidding across the floor until I crashed headfirst into the tripod. Benny rushed over and grabbed the camera as the tripod tipped over and tore into the seamless backdrop, ripping it open.

"What the fuck!" I heard Ida say as I lay on the floor. "Now look what you've done."

I resisted the impulse to correct her and tell her that it was actually Howard, not me, who had done it, and waited for whatever was going to happen next to happen. I didn't have to wait long.

"Get him off the floor," Benny said. "Put him in a chair."

Howard grabbed my legs and dragged me across the floor toward a chair. Then he grabbed me by the shoulders, lifted me up off the floor, and dropped me into a chair. I was surprised I could still breathe because my nose seemed to be missing. My face felt wet with blood.

"You look like shit," Benny said. "You know that?"

I didn't need a mirror to answer that one, so I just nodded.

"You want a glass of water?"

"Thanks," I said, trying to smile.

"Pumpkin, would you get our guest a glass of water?"

"Sure, hon, no problem."

I heard the door open as Ida stepped out of the room. Benny pulled up a chair and sat down.

"Okay, what do you say we start over?"

"Does that mean he's gonna hit me again?" I said, nodding at Howard.

Benny grinned. "That's funny," he said. "You're a funny guy." He glanced at Howard. "We're good, Howard. You can take off now."

"You sure you don't want me to hit him again?" Howard said, sounding disappointed.

Benny shook his head, then looked at me. "I think he got the message."

I wasn't sure exactly what the message was. Maybe that I never should have shown up in the first place.

"I can always come back if you need me," Howard said.

"I'll let you know. Just one thing, Howard…" Benny said.

Howard looked up at Benny and waited for the rest of it.

"You're gonna forget what you heard here today, right?"

"Soon as I walk out the door, Mr. Velasco. But I can't wait to see the pic on the wall. Makes me kinda proud, you know?"

"Keep your nose clean, Howard," Benny said. "Wouldn't want your bail to get revoked now, would we?"

"No, sir," Howard said, and headed for the door.

"Hey Howard," I said.

Howard turned and looked at me, his face twisted with suspicion. "Yeah? What do you want?"

"Can I talk to you for a minute?"

Howard traded glances with Benny, as if unsure of his next move.

"It's okay, Howard. See what the man wants."

Howard came up to me. "Okay, talk," he sneered, "if you can."

"Just got one thing to say to you," I said, as I managed to lift myself out of the chair.

"Yeah, what's that?"

I punched him in the stomach as hard as I could under the circumstances.

"Payback," I said, then sank back into the chair.

Howard grunted and doubled up, then grabbed the chair to keep himself from collapsing on the floor. Benny smiled, as though he was impressed. Or maybe he just liked to see the fights from the comfort of his office. Howard's face was red and contorted with rage. Saliva was dripping out of his mouth. He straightened up and lunged at me, fist clenched, and I braced myself for another round. But Benny stopped him cold.

"That's enough for today, Howard."

"He hit me!" Howard complained, like he was ten years old.

Benny shrugged. "You hit him first."

"It was a sucker punch," Howard said.

Benny paused, then nodded at the wall of inmates on parole. "You want your picture on the wall, Howard?"

Howard nodded.

Benny smiled. "Close the door on your way out."

Howard glared at me, then walked out of the office. Benny turned to me.

"Not bad," he said. "Didn't know you had it in you."

Neither did I, I thought, but sometimes enough was enough. And getting worked over by some mook on parole was way more than enough. Moments later, Ida returned with a glass of water.

"Thanks," I said, as I wrapped my hands around the glass.

I tried to take a sip, but my mouth wouldn't

cooperate. The water dribbled down my chin and onto my clothes. I didn't mind, though. Maybe it would wash off some of the blood.

"Okay," Benny said, taking the glass out of my hands. "You want to run that past me again? Why exactly do I want to help 'em jump bail?"

"Because they're dead otherwise."

"What do you care?"

"They did me a favor. They shouldn't have to die for it."

Benny nodded. "Loyalty, I like that. You want to protect 'em, right?"

"Not just them," I said.

A sly smile spread across Benny's face. "You too, huh?"

I nodded.

"And maybe Daphne, too."

I said nothing. He knew the answer to that one.

"You got the ten percent?"

I shook my head. Benny scowled at me.

"You're fuckin' kidding me. I gotta put up the ten percent and then take it in the shorts on the rest?"

"You'll get first cut at the cash soon as I find it. I promise."

Benny scoffed. "Promise? You don't even know where it is."

"Yeah, but she does," Ida said in a deadly tone of voice.

"Ida's right. Just give me some time, that's all I need."

Benny looked down at his hands, then looked up at Ida.

"What do you think, pumpkin?"

"Give him a little time, hon...but not too much time."

Benny nodded. "You heard the lady. You got a little time, but if you try to run out on us, I'm gonna have to put a skip tracer on you. You know what a skip tracer is, Max?"

"Yeah, I know what a skip tracer is."

I'd learned a bit about crime hanging out with Nicole, and I knew that skip tracers were bounty hunters who chased down inmates when they missed their court dates. If Benny sent one after me. I knew it would hurt.

"Okay then," Benny said, clapping me on the shoulder. "Glad we're on the same page."

Then, out of the blue, Ida said, "You fucking her yet?"

I looked at her with what I guessed was a startled expression. "Excuse me?"

"You not gonna find out what she knows 'til you fuck her."

"Right," I said, not knowing what else to say.

Benny offered a leering smile. He nodded at Ida. "Guess you better get to work, eh?"

Ida called Terri into the office to start the paperwork. She pretended not to notice my bruises or the blood on my face as Benny filled her in on the details. Once the paperwork was complete, Benny informed me, he would contact the jail where Ernie and Janelle were being held and post the bail amount. Then, like it said on the door, they would be out on bail and scot-free. Seeing how it was Sunday afternoon, however, it would probably be Monday before their bail applications would be processed and they were released.

They let me go after that. Judging by the shocked

looks on their faces, I figured I must've scared the daylights out of everybody in the waiting room when I stepped out of the office and walked to the door. But that was nothing compared to how much I scared myself when I got home and looked in the mirror.

Chapter 14

I was in the bathroom trying to put my face back together when the doorbell rang. The sound caught me by surprise. I threw a glance in the direction of the door, even though I was down the hall and nowhere near it. I hadn't buzzed anybody into the building, so who was it and how did they get in, I wondered. But company was the last thing I wanted. Judging by the state of my face, I'd had all the social interaction I could stand for one day. I wasn't sure I'd survive another round.

But somebody was out there, waiting in the hallway outside my apartment, and whoever it was rang the bell again, just to remind me. I looked at myself in the mirror and decided that whoever was out there would just have to deal with it.

I stepped to the door and opened it, and saw her standing there. I could tell by the look on her face that what she saw shocked her.

"What happened to your face?"

"Don't ask."

"I just did."

I nodded, conceding the point.

"Can I come in?"

I stepped aside and she walked into the living room. She wore a T-shirt and jeans with her cellphone tucked into her butt like a teenager.

"How'd you get into the building?"

"The manager let me in."

"Cornell?"

"Is that his name?"

I smiled. She didn't need to know his name. All she needed to do was work her magic.

She looked around the room, then turned to me. "I told him I was worried about you and he let me right in."

"Just like that, huh?"

"I hope you don't mind me stopping by like this, Max. I just got worried when I didn't hear from you."

Was she kidding? She could've stopped by anytime, 24/7, and that was the part that scared me. And the part that made me want more of her.

"I was busy," I said.

"Doing what—getting beat up?" she said, with a sly smile.

"It's a long story," I said.

"I love long stories," Daphne said, settling herself on the sofa. She glanced at the records that lined one wall in my living room. "Last time I was here you said it was too late to play a record. How about now?"

"Sure, what do you want to hear?"

Daphne shrugged. "Whatever you want to play for me."

I walked over to the record case and started browsing. What would be right for her, for us, for this moment, I wondered. I was used to putting on headphones and losing myself in the music. But now I was losing myself in Daphne.

"How many do you have?"

"I don't know, a couple thousand, maybe."

"Must be hard to keep track of 'em all."

"Yeah, sometimes it is."

"Wouldn't it be easier to just listen to some online streaming service or something?"

I paused. "I guess it would be, but it wouldn't be the same."

You couldn't touch streaming the way you could touch a record. You couldn't see the cover art or read the liner notes. And you couldn't listen to the music the way it was originally recorded, the way it was meant to be heard by the musicians who created it. Records were time machines that let you drop a needle on the past.

I wanted to explain it all to her, and yet I knew there was no way I could ever explain it. So I decided to let the music speak for itself. I pulled out an album and put it on the turntable. The sounds of a jazz trio from back in the sixties filled the room.

"That's beautiful," Daphne said. Then she changed the subject. "So what happened to you?"

I gave myself a moment to collect my thoughts. Daphne didn't need to hear about Benny and Ida Velasco, and their claims on the money. But Ernie and Janelle were another story. They'd done her a favor, and were about to pay for it with their lives.

"You remember Ernie and Janelle?" I said.

She looked up at me. "Ernie and Janelle?"

She said it like she'd never heard of them.

"They cleaned up, remember?"

"Oh right. Sorry, I'm terrible with names."

Like it never happened, I thought. Ernie and Janelle had that one right.

"What about them?" Daphne said. "Did they beat you up?"

I smiled and shook my head, then sat down next to her. "They're in trouble."

"Is this the long story you were gonna tell me?"

I nodded, then braced her on how the cops had found a gun in the car when they pulled Ernie and Janelle over for speeding. They were arrested and charged with unlawful possession. Now that they were facing felony charges, Rikers wanted them bailed out so they could be hit before they copped a plea, which, as I explained to Daphne, would take us all down.

"Rikers?"

I nodded.

"Oh, you don't have to worry about him."

"I don't?"

Daphne shook her head. "Mick and Janis are on the case."

"Seriously? A couple of hippies from the Haight? You really think they're gonna go through with it?"

"Yeah, sure. They need the money. They've got a kid on the way."

Murder for the good of the family, I thought. A baby born of parents with blood on their hands from day one.

"They just need to know where to find him."

I looked at Daphne. "Is that why you're here?"

Daphne smiled. "Not the only reason, silly. If that was all I wanted I could've just called you."

Then she leaned in and kissed me, and the world as I knew it faded away, and all that mattered was her tongue slithering into my mouth like a snake.

She took her clothes off by the window so I could watch. Shed her jeans and T-shirt and bra and panties in the slanting afternoon sunlight that lay in stripes across her body and made her seem like some wild jungle creature. And maybe she was. But I was in that jungle with her. I could hear the hum of life on Valencia Street, but it was miles away from where we were.

I pulled her close and hot tears spilled onto her breasts.

"You okay?" I said.

Daphne nodded. I could feel the heat of us, flesh to flesh.

"You sure?" I said.

Daphne put an index finger to my lips and then silenced me with a kiss. And when she shuddered and cried out, I wanted the moment to last forever, even though I knew it was already fleeting. Afterward, we lay in each other's arms, sweating, breathing, not knowing what to say.

Then Daphne sat up and looked at me. She shook her head and smiled to herself. "I haven't been with anybody since Archie…I never imagined it would be with the guy who wrote his obituary."

I smiled. "I wonder if he's looking down on us."

"I hope not," Daphne said. "I hate being watched."

"You sure?"

She gave me a teasing smile. "Depends who's watching, I guess."

I pulled her close and kissed her. I wanted to watch her forever, and I figured she could see it in my eyes. It scared me, but not enough to stop me. We fell asleep in each other's arms, then a car alarm on Valencia woke me a little after six. I felt for her next to me, but there was no one there. I wondered if she'd left without saying goodbye. I got up and went into the living room and saw her by the window. She was wrapped in a towel and watching the rush of life on the street that made the Mission one of the city's most vibrant neighborhoods.

She saw me and smiled. "I borrowed a towel. I hope

127

you don't mind."

"I don't mind," I said, flashing on how she was wrapped in a bathrobe the first time I saw her.

"I always wanted to live in the city. Did I ever tell you that?"

"Yeah, you did."

Daphne smiled. "Sorry."

"I was afraid you'd left."

"Without saying goodbye?"

"Something like that."

She came up to me and kissed me, and I could feel the heat coming off her body in waves.

"I'd never leave without saying goodbye, Max, not after today. Anyway, we need to talk, remember?"

I remembered, even though I didn't want to. I remembered like I remembered Roy and Donny. But maybe it was better this way. With Rikers gone, maybe things could go back to normal and we could stop talking about who we needed to kill next.

"About Mick and Janis, right?" I said.

"We don't want to wait too long. They might change their minds and then we'd have to do it."

I wasn't sure she'd mind if that happened. She already pulled the trigger twice, why not make it a trifecta?

"He likes to go to midnight movies at the Roxie," I said, as the shame rose up inside me.

"The Roxie?"

"It's a movie theater on 16th Street and Valencia." I opened a drawer and took out the mugshot of Rikers that Nic had given me and handed it to Daphne. "They're gonna need this."

Daphne studied Rikers's face, then shook her head.

"Not my type."

Did that matter, I wondered. What if Rikers was her type? Would that have meant she would've been happy to screw him, not shoot him?

Then, our business re: death and desire apparently concluded, she looked up at me and said, "I guess that's it, then. I better get dressed."

"You're leaving?"

"Kim wants to talk about offers."

"On Sunday?"

Daphne shrugged. "She's hungry. You know what it's like to be hungry, don't you, Max?"

I pulled her into my arms and kissed her hard on the mouth. I was hungry, all right, but it was the kind of hunger that could never be satisfied, that always left you wanting more until it was too late.

I tried to push what I had done out of my mind. But as I sat at my desk and browsed through the background materials of the recently departed, it was hard to forget that if Rikers joined their ranks, I had helped make it happen. Who would write his obit, I wondered. Would he even get one? Or would he be just another refrigerated corpse on a slab down at the morgue? He was a snitch, though, which I figured counted for something. It just wasn't enough to keep him alive. But I was getting ahead of myself. Daphne and I had set it up, but there was no guarantee that Mick and Janis would follow through.

Then the Ripper came up to my desk and changed the subject. "This one's still warm, mate," he said, and dropped a manila folder on my desk with a thud. "Get it done as soon as you can."

I looked up at him. "Who's dead?"

"Some rockstar."

I opened the folder and scanned the cover sheet. "Gary and the Gladiators?"

Dickie shrugged.

"So what's the rush?"

"Mac was a fan back in the day," Dickie said, referring to Ross MacDonald, the *Bugle's* managing editor. "Saw the Gladiators on tour, got their autographs, even bought one of their gladiator outfits on eBay."

"Did he like wear it to concerts?"

The Ripper's face turned sour. "I say, why don't you ask him the next time you see him? I'm sure he'd love to tell you all about it. Maybe he'll show you pictures and play some of their records for you. In the meantime, he wants to see this obit in print sooner rather than later."

"Got it," I said.

Dickie nodded and walked away. I turned to the background materials and learned that a faded seventies metal star named Gary Dunham, who, with his band, Gary and the Gladiators, liked to perform in Roman gladiator outfits, had dropped dead onstage at some casino in Florida during an oldies tour. I'd never heard of the guy. Then again, I'd never heard of most of the people whose lives I memorialized in 800 words or less. I was a stranger writing about strangers. We'd never get to know each other, and in a way we were both trapped in our versions of oblivion.

I scanned Dunham's file, which included photos of Gary and the band in full gladiator drag, jotted down some notes, then picked up the phone. Background materials were useful, but my time on the obits desk had taught me that family and friends could help celebrate a person's life in ways that documents never could. And that, of course, was the point of an obituary—to bring to life a life that was lost. But who were we kidding? We didn't bring anybody back to life. They were dead to begin with and they stayed that way. Mostly.

I punched in a number and waited until a woman answered.

"Mrs. Dunham? This is Max McQuinn from the *Bay Area Bugle*. I'm working on your husband's obituary."

"Oh yeah. I guess you want to talk about Gary, huh?"

"Yes, if you don't mind."

"No, I don't mind."

"I know this is a difficult time. I'm sorry for your loss and I appreciate you taking my call."

I began every call with survivors this way, hoping that an expression of sympathy and respect would encourage the friend or relative to talk openly about the deceased. But the more I did so, the more I worried about coming off as a phony, apologizing for a loss that meant nothing more to me than a deadline. And yet, what else was there to say?

"What would you like to know?"

"What do you think would be the best words to describe your husband?"

I heard her chuckle. "He rocked. Right up until the end."

"I wanted to ask you about the band's name and the outfits. How did all that happen?"

"Oh my God, the outfits. Gary loved all those old Hollywood gladiator movies. He thought it would be fun to have the band dress up like gladiators."

"Where did he get the outfits?"

"Back then he heard about some fire sale at a studio that used to make gladiator movies and he bought up all the outfits."

"How did the band like wearing them?"

"I think Gary was the only who was really into it. The rest of the guys went along with it because it was either wear 'em or you're out." Dunham paused. "He just wanted to be different, you know?"

I studied the photos of the band. "Well, I'd say he pulled it off, right?"

"Yeah, he sure did." Dunham paused, then said, "You want to hear a funny story?"

"Sure."

"Gary used to get pictures from fans and they were all wearing gladiator outfits too. He got a big kick out of that."

"That is funny," I said. I imagined the memories rushing through her as she spoke.

She fell silent for a few moments, and I wondered if I'd lost the call.

"I don't think I want to talk anymore right now," Dunham said, breaking the silence. "I'm just really missing him a lot right now, you know. Is that okay?"

"Of course," I said. "Thanks for your time. I appreciate it."

I never knew how a call with the next of kin would turn out. Sometimes they were happy to talk about the deceased, as if talking about them made it seem like they were still alive. Other times they started off eager to share memories, but soon found themselves overcome by their grief. I figured that there was a lot his widow could have told me about the late Gary Dunham, but none of it would have brought him back onstage.

I hung up the phone and jotted down the lede: "Gary Dunham, Rock 'n' Roll Gladiator, Dies Onstage at 69."

It was the kind of lede that I figured the Ripper would like. I hoped Mac would like it too. I read it over just to make sure I was good with it, then began working on the copy for Dunham's obit. I'd just finished a draft when my cellphone vibrated. I glanced at the screen and saw it was Benny Velasco.

"They're getting out today," Benny said, cutting to the chase.

"Okay, thanks."

"You know where to go?"

"Yeah."

"What are you gonna do with them?"

"I don't know, keep 'em alive."

Benny scoffed. "You better worry about keeping yourself alive."

The line went dead. I checked my watch, then sent the draft to the Ripper and texted Nicole.

Chapter 15

I nosed the car into a parking space across the street from the SF County Jail's Intake and Release Center and killed the engine. It was the middle of the day and the weather was good, even better if you were getting out of jail. Deputies, guards, and staff were streaming out of the building for lunch. According to Benny Velasco, nobody did time at the center. Inmates were housed there for the time it took to complete their booking or release processes. Ernie and Janelle were on their way out, which is why Nicole and I were there.

"How long is this gonna take? What if Dan sees me?" Nicole said, referring to Dan Bellamy, her ex and the SFPD detective with whom she shared Rikers as a CI.

I checked my watch. "They should be coming out any time now." I looked at her. "Why? You got a date?"

"Very funny. I've got a deadline, and by the way, so do you." She looked out at the building. "We should be doing our jobs, not running a taxi service for inmates."

"C'mon, Nic. We've been over this, okay?"

She turned away from the window. "Rikers thinks we're gonna whack 'em. What happens when we don't?"

"What does he expect? That we're just gonna gun 'em down the minute they walk out the door? You tell me. He's your snitch, not mine," I said.

"I don't know what to expect besides trouble.

What's gonna happen when he finds out that we didn't do it?"

"Maybe the hippies will get to him first."

"Have you heard from her?"

"Daphne?"

"Who else?"

"I saw her last night."

Nicole offered a sly smile. "And?"

I felt the shame rush into my face. "I told her they could find Rikers at the Roxie," I said quietly.

"I guess that didn't feel good, huh?"

I looked sharply at Nicole. "What do you think?"

Nicole lowered her eyes. "Sorry," she said, a chastened look on her face. "I'm sure it sucked."

"Yeah, it did."

"So what exactly are you doing with her?"

"You mean besides helping her kill people?"

"Maybe this'll be the end of it," Nicole said.

"Yeah, maybe," I said, wishing I could believe it.

"What if it isn't?"

Out of the corner of my eye I saw a crowd of inmates walk out of the Intake and Release Center. Then I saw Ernie and Janelle. They stood on the sidewalk and traded glances as the crowd dispersed around them.

"Heads up," I said. "They're out."

Nicole followed my line of sight. "That's them?"

I nodded. "Roll down the window."

Nicole rolled down the window as I turned the key and started the car. I waited for the traffic on 7th Street to clear, then hung a U-turn and pulled up in front of Ernie and Janelle. I saw Ernie smile, like maybe he recognized the car.

I leaned across Nicole and said, "Get in."

Nicole stepped out of the car. Inmates were milling around the entrance, waiting for rides or maybe deciding where to go next now that they were out. I could see her face tighten as she pushed the seat forward so Ernie and Janelle could climb into the back seat. But it was clear from their puzzled expressions they had no clue who she was or why they should get in the car.

Nicole stood awkwardly by the door and looked around. I could tell she was worried someone like her ex might see her hanging out with a couple of inmates. Not that I could blame her. I didn't much like it myself.

I saw Ernie and Janelle trade glances, as if they were still trying to put it together. I noticed that Janelle wore the same sullen expression as the first time I saw her. Apparently, getting out of jail hadn't improved her outlook on life. Then again, cleaning up crime scenes wasn't exactly the kind of work that would make anybody smile.

An SF Sheriff's Department bus with bars on the windows pulled up in front of the center. The door hissed open and sheriff's deputies stepped off the bus, then led a line of handcuffed inmates into the center.

Nicole saw them and leaned into the car. "We need to go, Max. Now," she insisted.

I nodded and leaned across the passenger seat toward the open door. "Hey Ernie, it's me, the clean-up in Marin the other night, remember?" I said.

His face lit up with recognition. "Oh yeah, right. What are you doing here?"

"I'll explain on the way," I said. "Get in the car."

Finally, Ernie and Janelle climbed into the back seat, then Nic got back in the car and pulled the door shut.

"So what's going on, man?" Ernie said as we drove

away. "What are you doing here? Who bailed us out?"

Nicole and I traded glances. I locked eyes with Ernie in the rearview.

"A friend bailed you out," I said.

"What friend?" Janelle asked in a suspicious tone of voice. "Rikers?"

Nicole turned around and looked at Ernie and Janelle. "A friend who's trying to keep you alive."

Ernie and Janelle exchanged shocked glances. But now Janelle didn't just look sullen, she also looked scared.

"What you talking about?" Ernie said. "Who the fuck are you?"

"We work together," I said.

"You're not making sense, man. What the fuck is going on?" Ernie said.

"You need to get out of town," I said. "Sooner rather than later."

"Why?"

"Because Rikers wants you dead, okay?" Nicole said sharply.

Ernie and Janelle stared back at her in stunned silence. Then Ernie scoffed.

"That's bullshit, man. What's he gonna want us dead for?"

"He's afraid you're gonna cop a plea on the guns, maybe tell 'em about the clean-up in Marin."

"We do that, we all go down," Janelle said.

"Including Rikers," Nicole said.

"So how come we're out?"

"Easier to hit us when we're out, right?" Janelle said.

Nicole and I exchanged glances.

"Where do you live?" I said.

"Oakland," Janelle said, her voice cracking, as if the shock made it hard to get the word out.

I headed down Bryant and jumped on the Bay Bridge. We were across the span and into the flatlands, rolling past the cranes and container yards at the Port of Oakland when I saw the truck. A black pickup filling my rearview. I'm not sure why I noticed it, maybe because I liked trucks, even though I'd never owned one. Or maybe I was just being paranoid and thought whoever was behind me had to be following me.

"What you lookin' at, man?" Ernie said after the third or fourth time I glanced in the mirror.

"Just checking out the traffic, that's all," I said.

I saw Ernie turn around and look out the rear window.

"Ain't nothing there. Just cars, man."

I nodded. "Yeah, just cars." I glanced in the mirror again and noticed that the truck was gone.

"It's you guys, right?" Janelle said.

I glanced at her in the rearview.

"It ain't Rikers who's gonna clip us. It's the two of you."

Nicole and I exchanged glances. She turned around and looked at Janelle. "Seriously? Is that what you think?"

"What else I'm gonna think? You the ones who picked us up."

"So we could kill you, right?" Nicole said.

"C'mon, girl," Ernie said, "they ain't down with that."

Janelle shrugged, unconvinced. "What you know, man?" she said. "All this time you be telling me we was tight with Rikers. You don't know nothin'." She turned and looked out the window.

"How the fuck was I supposed to know?" Ernie said.

Janelle whipped around to Ernie. I glanced in the rearview and saw the shine of tears in her eyes.

"You were supposed to know, okay? You were supposed to know!"

Ernie put his arm around her and pulled her close. "It's gonna be okay, girl," he said gently. "Everything gonna be okay."

I hoped to hell he was right. I glanced in the mirror again to see if my phantom pickup had reappeared. But there was still no sight of it. Twenty minutes later I pulled up in front of a rundown apartment building south of the interstate on International Boulevard.

"Get what you need," I said as Ernie and Janelle climbed out of the car. "But make it fast."

Nicole watched them walk into the building, then turned to me like there was something to say. But there wasn't, and we both knew it. After what seemed like an eternity, Ernie and Janelle emerged from the building with a couple of battered suitcases. We put them in the trunk and drove away.

The streets were thick with traffic by the time I pulled up in front of the bus station on San Pablo. I got out of the car and opened the trunk. Ernie joined me and we pulled out the suitcases.

"Thanks, man," he said. "I owe you one."

I shook my head. "I owed you one."

Ernie smiled. "We call it even then."

"Fair enough," I said. I grabbed my wallet and pulled out some cash and gave it to Ernie.

Ernie shook his head. "You don't need to do that,

man."

"Yeah, I do," I said. "And you're gonna need it."

Ernie took the cash and shoved it in his pocket.

I looked around, then nodded at the bus station. "Go," I said.

Ernie nodded, then he and Janelle headed toward the entrance, pulling their suitcases behind them. I closed the trunk, then climbed in behind the wheel.

"You think they're gonna be okay?" Nicole said as she watched Ernie and Janelle.

"I hope so," I said as I turned the key and the engine fired. "We've done all we can."

"Was it enough?"

"Is anything ever enough?" I said, locking eyes with Nicole. I checked traffic, then hung a U-turn on San Pablo Avenue.

That was when I saw it, the pickup truck I had seen on the freeway. Was it the same one? Pickups were the best-selling vehicles in America, and there had to be hundreds if not thousands of them on the road in the Bay Area.

I got my answer when I saw the truck slow as it approached the bus station. Suddenly I had a bad feeling.

I pulled over and looked out at Ernie and Janelle, who were almost at the door.

"Run!" I shouted. I left the engine running as I threw open the door and jumped out of the car. "Run!" But I was drowned out by the roar of traffic in both directions.

Nicole leaned out and looked sharply at me. "What?"

Seconds later, somebody inside the truck started shooting, raking the bus station with gunfire. Passengers heading in and out of the station jerked backward and sideways, then collapsed on the sidewalk as the rounds slammed into them. The lucky ones abandoned their luggage and ran screaming down the street.

Mission accomplished, the killer truck vanished as quickly as it had appeared. Then, as passengers scattered, I saw Ernie and Janelle. They were lying side by side, crumpled on the sidewalk in an ever-widening pool of blood. One of their suitcases had opened and the blood was seeping into the clothes that had spilled out onto the street. Nicole gasped. Her hand flew to her mouth. I saw her eyes widen with sheer horror.

"No…no…no," she said, shaking her head, as if she could will away what she had seen. She buried her face in her hands and slumped against the door. I could hear the muffled sounds of her saying "No" over and over, like a mantra for the dead.

It was time to go. I got back in the car, dropped the trans into first and pulled out into traffic. Nicole sat up and looked at me.

"Where are you going? We can't just leave them like that—"

"We have to get out of here, Nic. Somebody might've seen us drop 'em off and jotted down the license."

"But we should do something—"

"We *did* do something, and it wasn't enough."

We both fell silent as the shock took over. We were rolling through traffic but I felt as if I was on autopilot, because all I could see were Ernie and Janelle bleeding out on the sidewalk. They had planned to buy a one-way ticket to wherever the money they had would take them. Instead, they caught the oblivion express, free of charge.

Nicole's cellphone rang, jolting both of us out of our

thoughts. She pulled the phone out of her purse and glanced at the screen.

"It's him," she said, "Rikers."

We traded glances, then Nic put the phone on speaker and took the call.

"Just wanted to say thanks," Rikers said.

"Thanks for what," Nicole said, "helping you kill them?"

"I knew you didn't have it in you, Knickers. Just needed you to get 'em out."

I saw Nicole's face turn white. She dropped the phone and looked at me. "Pull over," she said.

"What?"

"Pull over!" she said, covering her mouth.

I swerved to the curb and stopped the car. Nicole pushed open the door and leaned out of the car, then threw up on the pavement. As I listened to her retching, it was as though I was listening to her body tear itself apart with rage and sorrow. She sat up and pulled the door closed, then wiped her mouth.

"We killed them," she said, staring straight ahead.

I shook my head. "Rikers killed them, Nic. We tried to help them."

Nicole turned to me and offered a bitter smile. "They're dead, Max. How did we help them?"

I locked eyes with her, then looked away. I could hear the sound of traffic rushing past the car.

"We need to take him out," Nicole said.

I turned to her. The bodies were starting to pile up. I wondered if maybe it got easier the more you did it. Practice always did make perfect.

"How many people we gonna help die, Nic?"

"It won't be over until he's dead. Don't you see

that?"

"I guess I just see dead people."

Nicole shrugged. "Maybe that's because you're an obituary writer."

My cellphone rang. I pulled it out of my pocket and glanced at the screen.

"The Ripper," I said.

"You better take it."

"Max McQuinn," I said, taking the call.

"What a coincidence," the Ripper said. "I used to know a chap named Max McQuinn, wrote obits for the *Bugle*."

I rolled my eyes. The Ripper had missed his calling. He could've killed in standup.

"Hey, Dickie, what's up?"

"I just passed by your office and happened to notice that the stack of manila folders I left on your desk hadn't gotten any smaller. That's what's up. You planning on coming back to work anytime soon?"

"On my way," I said.

We were about to walk into the building when Nicole put her hand on my arm to stop me. She hadn't said a word on the ride back to work, and we had walked from the garage to the office in silence. But now when I looked at her, I could see it in her eyes, all the horror, grief and guilt that was consuming her.

"How do we do this, Max?"

"Do what?"

"Go back to work, like nothing happened."

"We just do it."

"That's it? Two people dead because of us?"

"We didn't kill them, Nic."

"We may as well have."

Robert Baty

She pushed past me and went into the building. The door closed behind us. When we got to the newsroom Nicole peeled off to the crime desk and I headed to obits. We each had our beats to cover, and somehow we had to find a way to live with what had happened and go on with our lives. Which meant we had a find a way to cover up our crimes, both to the police and to ourselves.

I ran into the Ripper on the way to my desk.

"Hey, look who's here," he said.

I managed a sheepish smile. "Hey, Dickie."

"I reckon you're about to put a dent in that stack of files on your desk, right, old chap?"

"Can't wait."

Dickie grinned. "That's what I like to hear."

I moved past him and headed toward the safety of my cubicle.

"By the way…"

I turned and waited for the rest of it.

"Mac liked your piece on the gladiator guy. Liked the way you spun the lede."

"Great. Thanks for letting me know."

Dickie nodded and moved on. And as I watched him walk across the newsroom to his office, I couldn't help wondering what the lede should be for Ernie and Janelle's double obit. Then I realized I still hadn't written Roy and Donny's obits. I was falling behind, and the body count was climbing.

Chapter 16

But I wasn't being paid to write their obits. I fired up my computer and went back to work. First on the list of the afternoon's obits was Raymond Treadway, who had died of a heart attack while riding a Powell Street cable car on his seventy-fifth birthday. Treadway was a retired supermarket executive who was famous for having founded the Golden Gate SuperSave chain. According to the background materials, Treadway had started out with a single mom-and-pop store in the Marina. From there he built a retail grocery empire that blanketed the Bay Area with stores.

There were pictures of Treadway standing proudly in front of the first store. They contrasted with other photos, taken later, of Treadway standing in front of one of his supermarkets. He looked older, but just as proud. I scanned the file, jotted down some notes, then reached out to Treadway's widow, Louise.

"Hello, Mrs. Treadway," I said, after Treadway's widow picked up. "This is Max McQuinn from the *Bay Area Bugle*. I'm working on your husband's obituary."

"Oh yes. Hello, Max. I suppose you want to talk about Raymond."

From the sound of her voice I guessed she was close to Treadway's age.

"Yes, if you don't mind."

"No, I don't mind. But please call me Louise."

"Sure, no problem," I said.

"What would you like to know?"

"What do you think would be the best words to describe your husband?"

I heard Louise chuckle. "Well, he was very ambitious. You could see that right from the start when he opened the first store."

"That was in the Marina, right?"

"Yes, that's right. It's still open, by the way."

"Yes, I know."

"Well, as soon as he opened the store he was thinking about the next one, and the one after that. He wanted to build an empire."

"Well, he succeeded, didn't he?" I said.

"Yes, he did. He was quite proud of that."

"What else was he proud of, would you say?"

"His cars, I suppose."

"His cars? Was he a collector?"

"Yes, he was. But he was very specific about what he collected."

"How so, if you don't mind me asking."

"He collected woodies, you know, station wagons with wood panels on the side."

I sat up straight and leaned into the call. I could feel my heart pick up the beat.

"Yes, I know what woodies are," I said.

"Ray loved woodies," Louise said. "Owned a whole fleet of 'em."

"Did he store them somewhere?"

"Yes, he belonged to a club called Woody Wonders. They stored the cars in a warehouse somewhere. They even had these funny little fridge magnets with the name of the club on them. Ray insisted on sticking them on the refrigerator."

I opened a desk drawer and took out the Woody Wonders fridge magnet I had found on Daphne's kitchen floor.

"Did you say Woody Wonders?" I said, looking at the magnet in the palm of my hand.

"Yes, have you heard of it?"

"It sounds familiar," I said. "Do you know where the warehouse was?"

"No idea. The cars were Ray's thing, not mine."

"What's going to happen to the cars now? Are you going to keep them?"

"Goodness, no. Not much point in keeping them now that's Ray's gone."

"Did Mr. Treadway ever mention a man named Archie Gibbs?"

"The gangster who just passed away?"

"Yes."

"Yes, as a matter of fact he did. Apparently, he collected woodies too. Ray told me he came to some of the meetings." Louise chuckled. "When he wasn't in jail that is." Louise paused. "Why do you ask? Are you suggesting that Ray was involved with a criminal?"

"No of course not," I said, wondering if perhaps I had gone too far. Writing an obituary was one thing; accusing the deceased of a crime was another. "I just heard somewhere that Gibbs was a collector. Seemed like a funny coincidence."

"That's life, Max. Just a series of funny coincidences and then it's over."

"Yes, I suppose you're right."

"By the way, are you sure you're a reporter? You sound more like a detective."

"I guess a good reporter has to be a little of both."

"I suppose," Louise said. "But I think I've said quite enough about my husband. More than I should have, perhaps."

"Sorry, I didn't mean to pry," I said.

Louise chuckled. "Of course you did. That's your job. Good day."

The line went dead. I rolled the magnet around in my hand, as if by doing so it would reveal its secrets. Maybe Louise Treadway was right. Maybe the fact that Archie and Raymond Treadway belonged to the same car club was just a coincidence. But why was I thinking there was more to it than that? Or was it that I needed it to be more than a coincidence?

And then I realized that it wasn't about coincidences at all. It was about the money. The Paycheck Today job. In the wake of all the blood in the street, and my role in trying to wash it away, I'd forgotten about the heist. But that was where it all began. If Raymond knew Archie, then maybe he knew about the money. Maybe Archie told him about it when they were hanging out at Woody Wonders, swapping stories about their cars. But it didn't add up. Why would Archie have confessed to a crime? Because he wanted to brag about how he got away with it. But it still didn't make sense to me. Even though I wanted it to make sense. Because if it never made sense, I'd never find the money. And if I never found the money, then Benny Velasco would send a skip tracer to find me.

I knocked out a draft of Treadway's obit and headlined it: 'Raymond Treadway, Founder of SuperSave Chain, Dies at 75.' Then I sent it along to the Ripper and called it a day. I swung by Nicole's desk on my way out of the building, but she'd left without saying goodbye or suggesting we drop by Dewey's for a drink. Not that I could blame her. It would take way more than a couple of rounds to forget the blood in the street. And even then, we'd see it all again once we sobered up.

I made myself a drink when I got home, then put on some tunes and let the music take me somewhere else. I left the lights off, then sat on the sofa and watched the room get dark around me. The darker it got the better I felt. I wanted to hide in the dark, but the trouble was I couldn't hide from myself. I figured Nicole felt the same way, and I wondered if she was hiding out too.

Then my phone beeped with a news alert and I realized I'd forgotten to set it to vibrate. The next mistake I made was reading the story. It was about a drive-by outside a Greyhound bus station in Oakland that left two people dead, and it took me out of the music and out of the dark.

I surfed to the *Bay Area Bugle* online and saw that Nicole's story about the shooting had been posted an hour ago. I tried to imagine how she felt covering a story in which she was not only a witness but also a participant. We had both broken one of the basic rules of journalism—never make the story about you. So far, we were the only ones who knew that. How long would it take before everyone at the *Bugle* knew it too?

My cellphone vibrated. I glanced at the screen and sighed. Her timing always was the best.

"I saw it on the news," Daphne said. "It was them, wasn't it, the ones who came to my house?"

"Yeah, it was them."

"What happened?"

"Rikers happened. I guess the happy couple haven't

149

found him yet."

"They're still looking. They'll find him."

"Whatever. It's a little late for Ernie and Janelle." The ice rattled in my glass as I knocked back the rest of my drink.

"Sounds like you're having a drink."

"Plural. Drinks."

"It's not your fault he killed them, Max."

"Whose fault is it, Daphne? They did you a favor and now they're dead."

"Are you blaming me?"

I scoffed. "Whose mess did they clean up?"

"I told you, it was self-defense. Why can't you believe me?"

I went into the kitchen and made myself another drink. "Doesn't matter whether I believe you," I said.

"It matters to me. There's a difference between murder and self-defense, isn't there?"

"Not to the dead there isn't," I said as I sipped my drink.

"Do you want me to come over? Maybe you shouldn't be alone right now."

"Who says I'm alone?" I glanced at the turntable. "The bar's open and the band's in the middle of their first set at the Black Hawk."

"Is that a no?"

An hour later I buzzed her into the building. Then came the knock on the door, and when I opened it everything I wanted and was afraid of wanting was standing there.

"Buy a girl a drink?" she said with a teasing smile, as I pulled her into my arms and closed the door behind her.

****

"What's gonna happen to us after, Max?"

We were laying in the dark together, her body next to mine. It didn't matter whether I could see her; I could feel her, sense her warmth rushing through me like a flame.

"After?"

"After this is all over."

"Will it ever be over?" I said.

"It has to be. Everything has an end, doesn't it?"

Including us, I thought, but maybe not yet.

"I guess if we're lucky we'll live happily ever after," I said with as much sarcasm as I could muster lying naked in the dark.

"Why not? Once Rikers is out of the way we'll be free, won't we?"

"Only if we get away with murder."

"People get away with murder all the time."

"What if we get caught?"

"We're too smart to get caught."

I wondered how many people doing hard time had told themselves the same thing just before the cuffs snapped shut around their wrists.

"I guess we'll have to wait and see."

"You don't believe me, do you?"

"I always want to believe you, Daphne. Isn't that enough?"

I heard Daphne giggle. She leaned over and kissed me.

"I guess so," she said. "But there's just one thing…"

"What's that?"

"We can't be happy until we find the money."

I smiled to myself. The bodies were piling up around

her, but that didn't mean she'd forgotten about the money. She didn't just need me to cover up after her whenever she had to shoot somebody; she also needed me to help her find the money. But the truth was I hadn't forgotten about it either. There was a part of me that wanted it, just like there was a part of me that wanted her.

"Remember when you told me that Roy and Donny weren't the only ones who were after the money?" I said.

"Yeah, I remember. Why?"

"You were right."

Daphne sat up in bed and turned on the lamp on the nightstand. The light fell across her breasts.

"What are you talking about?" she said.

"The names Benny and Ida Velasco mean anything to you?"

Her face tightened. She pulled the sheet up around her breasts, which made me regret having brought up Benny and Ida. It was a like a spell had been broken, and whoever we were and whatever we talked about when we were still in the dark was gone.

"She's Archie's ex-wife. What about her?"

"They want their cut, her and Benny."

"What do you mean, they want their cut?"

"Like you said, Roy and Donny weren't the only ones."

"I don't understand...how do you know about them?"

"They know about me, Daphne. They saw Archie's obit and now they want what's coming."

Daphne's face hardened. I figured that was how she looked when she pulled the trigger. Twice.

"They got nothing coming, okay?" she said, her eyes

flashing with defiance. "Nothing!"

She grabbed her clothes and started getting dressed. Things always looked different when you turned the lights on, I thought. Especially when it came to somebody else's money.

"It's not that simple," I said.

"Why not?"

"Because I'm on the hook for it, that's why."

"What do you mean?"

"Benny and Ida ate the cost of bailing out Ernie and Janelle, and they're not gonna get it back because dead people don't show up for their court dates."

"What's that got to do with you?"

"I made the deal with them."

"What's the deal?"

"They get a cut of the money when we find it."

"The money?" Daphne said sharply. "You mean my money, don't you?"

"They did you a favor, Daphne. The least we could do was try to save their lives."

"You should have asked me before you started giving away my money."

"There wasn't time. And if your happy hippies had done the job you said they were gonna do, Ernie and Janelle wouldn't be dead."

Daphne stepped into her flats and walked out of the bedroom. I followed her into the living room. She turned and looked at me and I could see the fury lighting up her eyes.

"Ida's not getting a dime of my money. I don't care what you promised them." She grabbed her coat and headed for the door.

"C'mon, Daphne, don't just walk out on me," I said,

grabbing her arm. "We need to talk about this."

"We just did," she said, shaking loose of me.

The door slammed behind her.

Chapter 17

I stayed up late after Daphne left, too wired to crawl into bed without her. I played records until the neighbors started pounding on the walls, then I tossed and turned for hours. As if I could somehow sleep her off. But Daphne was her own kind of bender, and I figured that the only guy who ever got over her was Archie, and he had to die to do it. Then around two in the morning, just after last call, somebody rang the buzzer. Was it her, I wondered. Was she back because she'd come to her senses and realized that we were doomed to be together? I wanted to believe it was her, and I did believe it was her all the way from my bedroom to the intercom by the front door.

But when I pushed the button, I heard Nicole say, "Meet me downstairs."

Ten minutes later we were in Nic's SUV, rolling through midnight streets to a midnight movie that never happened. Her portable scanner was on, squawking out calls for police, fire, and emergency medical services.

"You gonna tell me what's going on, Nic? What are we doing out here in the middle of the night?"

"There was a shooting at the Roxie," she said, as she headed up Valencia. "I heard it on the scanner."

I looked at her. "Rikers?"

"I don't know. Maybe."

Then she hung a left on 16th and we pulled up in

155

front of the Roxie Theater. The street was crowded with SFPD black-and-whites and emergency vehicles. Uniforms were taping off the theater's entrance with yellow crime scene tape. Flashing red and blue lights swept the block. Some of the locals who lived in the apartment buildings around the theater had come out in their bathrobes and pajamas. They huddled by the tape with their smartphones, maybe hoping to catch a glimpse of something they could post on social media.

A white van with the words "San Francisco Medical Examiner" was parked at the curb. The rear doors were open and two forensic techs were wheeling a gurney into the theater. There was an ambulance parked next to the van, and a hunky homicide detective was standing next to it. His name was Dan Bellamy, and in addition to being on the murder beat, he was also Nicole's married ex. Bellamy's partner, a stocky black woman named Robinson, was there too, and the two of them were talking to a security guard I remembered from the last time we went to a midnight movie at the Roxie. The guard was sitting in the back of the ambulance while paramedics bandaged his arm.

I glanced at the marquee and saw that Dario Argento's supernatural horror classic, "Suspiria," was on the bill. The copy informed me that once I'd seen the movie I'd never again feel safe in the dark. I already didn't feel safe in the dark. I didn't need a movie to scare me.

Nicole nosed into a parking spot down the block and we climbed out of the car and headed toward the theater. As we approached, two uniforms escorting a woman in handcuffs came out of the theater. She was sobbing and covered with blood.

I nudged Nicole and said, "Janis."

She stopped and looked at me. "As in Mick and Janis?"

I nodded. The cops escorted Janis to a black-and-white, then put her in the back seat and closed the door.

"Where's Mick, I wonder," Nic said.

Moments later, the two forensic techs emerged from the theater pushing the gurney. Only now there was a body bag on it. Nic and I exchanged glances, then watched the techs as they rolled the gurney to the van, slid it into the back and closed the doors.

"There's Mick," I said.

Nicole looked at me. "How do you know?"

I didn't know for sure who was in the bag, but Janis' tears and the blood on her clothes gave me a pretty good idea.

Just then Bellamy saw Nicole and came up to us.

"Hey Nicole," he said, "what are you doing here?"

"Same thing you're doing here, Dan," Nicole said.

Bellamy grinned, then looked at me like he was trying to place me. "McQuinn, right? Max McQuinn?"

I nodded. "That's right."

"You're on the obits desk."

"Right again."

"On deadline with the dead, huh?"

"Something like that."

"So what happened, Dan?" Nicole said.

"This couple came in like they were Bonnie and Clyde, tried to take out a mutual acquaintance."

"Rikers?" Nicole said.

Bellamy nodded.

"Is he dead?"

Bellamy shook his head. I tried to hide my

disappointment.

"Not a scratch," Bellamy said. "But the shooter's dead. Poor bastard couldn't aim worth a shit." He nodded at the security guard sitting in the back of the ambulance. "Winged the guard instead. He returned fire, double-tapped the shooter in the head." Bellamy tapped his forehead with his index and middle fingers.

"I saw a woman come out in handcuffs," Nicole said.

Bellamy nodded. "His girlfriend. She didn't even try to get away. Had to pull her off the body. We'll interview her, see if we can come up with a motive. We recovered the gun, so we'll see if we can trace it."

Dread uncoiled in the pit of my stomach. If Daphne's prints were still on the gun, they'd trace them back to her. And then they'd start asking questions. At least Janis was too distraught to recognize me when the cops brought her out of the theater. Then I remembered that my prints were on the gun too. I'd grabbed it that day by the pool with Mick and Janis because Daphne with a gun in her hand was enough to scare anybody. Given how things had turned out, I probably should've let her keep it. I thought I was doing the right thing, which was always a mistake. Instead, I'd incriminated myself.

"Bellamy!" Robinson shouted.

Bellamy looked up and saw Robinson requesting his presence.

"Gotta run, guys," he said. Then he looked at Nicole, and his voice seemed to soften. "Good to see you, Nicole. Hope I don't have to wait until somebody gets killed before I see you again."

"Give my best to your wife," Nicole said.

Bellamy flashed a tight smile, then moved away.

"That must've hurt," I said as we walked back to the car.

Nicole's face hardened. "So did finding out he was married."

"Too bad he missed," I said, as Nicole and I drove away from the theater.

"I told you they'd blow it," she said as we rolled through the Mission just before last call. "What do hippies know about killing people?"

I said nothing. I could see drunks stumbling out of the bars along Valencia, rubbing their eyes and staring up at the sky as if they'd just woken up.

"What if Janis talks?" I said. "You know what's gonna happen if she talks? She doesn't know about you, but she knows about me. She'd have no trouble picking me out of a lineup."

"She knows about Daphne too," Nicole said.

"Yeah, everybody knows about Daphne."

Nicole glanced at me and shook her head. "You sure know how to pick 'em, Max."

I shrugged. "I think she picked me."

"Lucky you." She paused for a beat, then said, "I don't suppose we can bail her out…"

"Janis?" I shook my head. "No way. Not on attempted murder and firearms charges."

I flashed on Scot Free Bail Bonds. No way Benny would agree to take it in the shorts again. Things had gone south ever since we made a deal, and if anybody was going to take it in the shorts it was going to be me. Nicole and I fell silent, but we didn't have to be mind readers to know what each other was thinking.

"What about Rikers?" Nicole said. "He got away

without a scratch. Who's gonna kill him now?"

I said nothing, just let it sink in, and the deeper it went the worse I felt.

Then Nicole said, "What about Daphne? Wasn't she supposed to do it?"

"Yeah, until she decided it would be fun to let the hippies do it."

"The cops have the gun she gave them," Nic said. "They'll trace the registration back to her. She'll go down for it."

"She's not the only one," I said.

Nic glanced at me.

"My prints are on the gun too."

Nicole's eyes widened. "What? How the hell did that happen?"

"Doesn't matter now," I said, flashing on the day by the pool when I was dumb enough to grab the gun out of Daphne's hands because I was afraid it might go off. Now it was about to blow up in my face.

"Like hell it doesn't. You better hope they rubbed off by now."

I looked at her. "What do you mean?"

"It's hard to lift latent prints off firearms."

"Why?"

"Because the surfaces are oily and dirty. Plus, you weren't the only one who touched it, so the multiple impressions would be smeared by the gun changing hands."

I smiled. "I guess it pays to know a crime reporter."

Nicole's cellphone vibrated inside her purse. She reached for it and glanced at the screen. Then she looked up at me and I knew right away who it was. She put the phone on speaker and set it in the cup holder. Then she pulled over and killed the engine and put the phone on speaker.

"Hey Knickers, you hear the news?"

"Yeah, I heard," Nicole said.

"Aren't you gonna ask me if I'm okay?"

"What do you want, Rikers?"

"I want to know who they were and how they knew where to find me."

Nicole and I exchanged glances.

"How should I know?" Nicole said. "Maybe they liked to go to the Roxie."

"You and Max know I like to go to the Roxie."

"You think we had something to do with it?"

I could feel my stomach tighten. He knew, the way that guys like him always knew the worst about people.

"Somebody was behind it," Rikers said. "Maybe it was Daphne. That's her name, right? Daphne?"

"Why don't you go ask her?" Nicole said.

"I don't want to ask her," Rikers said. "I want you to take her out. Just like she tried to take me out."

This is where I came in, I thought. First Daphne toyed with killing Rikers. Then she farmed it out to Mick and Janis. Now Rikers wanted us to kill her. It wasn't spin the bottle, but it was close. More like spin the gun.

"You want us to kill her?" I said.

"Yeah, I want you to kill the bitch. You got a problem with that?"

"We've all got a problem with that, Rikers."

"What's the fuckin' problem?" Rikers said, his voice tight with annoyance.

"We kill her we don't get the money."

Nicole stared at me, her eyes wide as saucers.

Rikers paused. "What money?"

161

"She's the only one who knows where it is," I said.

"What the fuck you talking about?"

"The loot from Archie's score. She knows where he hid it."

"Who the fuck's Archie?"

I smiled to myself. This was easier than I thought. I saw Nicole shake her head in disbelief. But it didn't matter whether she believed it, it only mattered if Rikers believed it long enough to keep Daphne alive.

"You never heard of Archie Briggs?" I said.

"Fuck Archie Briggs. What about the money?"

"Archie pulled an armored car heist before he died. But nobody knows what he did with the money. Except Daphne."

"So where is it?"

"I'm working on it, Rikers. But here's the thing. If we take her out, we're never gonna find it. You get my drift?"

Rikers fell silent. Nicole mouthed "What the fuck are you doing?" I held up my hand to stop her. Then Rikers came on again and said, "We need to talk. Now. And not on the phone. I'll text you the address. See you there."

Moments later, an address appeared on Nicole's phone. We exchanged glances, then Nicole started the car.

"I hope you know what you're doing," she said.

"So do I."

"Maybe we should talk to Dan."

I looked at her, wondering if I heard her right. "And tell him what?"

"Just come clean about what happened."

"Sure, that's a great idea, Nic. Let's all go to jail for

the next ten years."

Nicole paused. "It's all about her, isn't it?" she said as she pulled away.

"What if it is? What's wrong with keeping her alive?"

"Nothing, unless it gets us killed. What do you think is gonna happen when Rikers finds out that nobody knows where the money is, or even if there is any money?"

"I don't know, haven't gotten that far."

"You should stick to dead people, Max. You're not too good with people who are still alive."

"You ready to kill her, Nic?"

Nicole paused. "I don't have a gun."

"I do," I said, flashing on the Glock I took off Tiffany's man from Rio.

Nicole glanced at me her eyes filled with surprise.

"Don't ask," I said.

Chapter 18

The used car lot was somewhere south of Market, on a deserted stretch of rundown mom and pop auto mechanics, upholstery shops, and car stereo stores. The sign above the lot read "Better Deals All Day." A rusty shipping container that served as an office sat in the middle of the lot, which was surrounded by a chain-link fence topped with barbed wire. As we pulled up, I noticed the gate was open.

"A used car lot?" Nicole said as we pulled up. "This can't be right." She grabbed her phone and checked the address that Rikers had sent her.

I shrugged. "Maybe he's selling cars on the side when he isn't snitching."

Nicole scoffed. "Seriously? Stealing cars would be more like it."

We got out of the car and looked around. But there wasn't much to see except a bunch of cars nobody wanted to buy. Then the headlights on a van facing the street came on. But whoever was behind the wheel remained hidden in the shadows. Nicole and I shielded our eyes, startled by the light. The headlights flashed twice.

"I guess that's our cue," I said.

"I don't like this, Max. What are we doing here, anyway? This is crazy. We don't even know who's in the van."

The headlights flashed again.

"I think we're about to find out."

Nicole and I walked down the driveway toward the van. Suddenly, the lights dimmed as the engine started. Then whoever was behind the wheel gunned the engine, as if the van was a muscle car and the driver wanted to impress us. But a van never impressed anybody, no matter how many times you gunned the engine. Nicole and I stopped. We traded glances, as if expecting to find an answer in each other's eyes. But all I saw was fear, and I hated that I was the reason she was scared. I had dragged her into it to save Daphne, and now through no fault of her own she was in as deep as I was.

Then the engine roared and the van rushed toward us. I saw it coming and pushed Nicole out of the way. We stumbled over a couple of cars and hit the ground. The van screeched to a halt with inches to spare. I felt myself break out in a cold sweat. I looked up at the van and saw a skinny blonde with a junkie's pallor behind the wheel. She was in her late twenties, I guessed, with tats and a choppy punk haircut with blue highlights.

"Scared 'em, didn't I baby." She grinned.

"Sure did," I heard Rikers say.

The door opened on the passenger side and he climbed out of the van. He wasn't alone, though. There was a gun in his hand.

"Hey guys, glad you could make it." He nodded at the blonde. "Say hi to Loretta."

I ignored the introduction and helped Nicole to her feet. Her face was bruised and her eyes were blazing with anger.

"You okay?" I said. It was a stupid question under the circumstances and Nicole ignored it. She was anything but okay.

She looked sharply at Rikers. "What the fuck, Rikers?" Then, without waiting for an answer, she glanced at Loretta. "You trying to kill us?

"We're just having a little fun," Loretta said.

"Is running people over in the middle of the night your idea of fun?" I said.

"You ain't dead, are you?"

"No thanks to you." I looked at Rikers. "What's up with the gun? You want tell us what's going on?"

Rikers pulled the van's side door open. "We're taking a ride."

"Excuse me?" Nicole said. "A ride where?"

"I'll tell you on the way. Get in," he said, motioning with the gun.

Nicole and I exchanged glances.

"What?" Nicole said, confused.

"You heard me," Rikers said. "Get in the van."

"No," Nicole said, shaking her head. "I'm not getting in your stupid van."

"The van's not stupid, bitch," Loretta said. "You're stupid."

I wondered where Rikers had found her. I figured maybe she came with the van when he stole it off the lot.

Rikers' face hardened. He came up to Nicole and jabbed the gun into her neck.

"You wouldn't dare," she said.

"You sure? Maybe you should ask Ernie and Janelle about that," he said.

I didn't like seeing a gun shoved into Nicole's neck. It was rude and showed a lack of respect.

"Don't do that," I said.

Rikers looked at me. "You want some too?"

"You heard me," I said, locking eyes with Rikers.

He swung the gun toward me. I didn't much like a gun in my face. I wrote obituaries. The dead were my beat, and the last time I checked they weren't armed. But lately it seemed as if more and more people were pointing guns at me.

"He's scared now, ain't he, baby?" Loretta said.

Rikers wanted me to be scared, but the truth was I was sick of being scared. Enough was enough. Rikers gave himself a moment to look back at Loretta and smile. Which was his first mistake. I made my move. I grabbed the gun by the barrel and yanked it toward me. Rikers stopped smiling and whipped around, his eyes filled with shock surprise.

"What the fuck!" he said as he struggled to hang on to the gun.

But I knew he could feel it slipping away from him. Another thirty seconds and the gun would be mine. Then Loretta had to go and spoil it.

"Freeze, asshole!" she shouted.

I looked up at her and saw yet another gun pointed in my direction. This one was a sleek, compact semiautomatic pistol. It was pink and no bigger than the palm of Loretta's hand.

"You like my girlfriend?" Loretta said. "She's cute, ain't she?" Loretta's finger was on the trigger and she was holding the gun with both hands. She looked like she knew how to use it. And probably wanted to.

Rikers grabbed the gun out of my hands and shoved the barrel into my neck. I figured that maybe it was his favorite move. Or maybe he'd seen it in a cop show on TV and wanted to try it out.

"What are you gonna do, Rikers?" I said. "Shoot us?

167

Then what?"

Rikers glared at me, because that was all he could do. The gun was a prop, and we both knew it. He waved it toward the van.

"Get in the fucking van, both of you."

I looked at Nicole. "Let's go, Nic."

We walked toward the van, then Nicole stopped and turned to Rikers.

"How many more people you gonna kill, Rikers?"

"As many as it takes to get what I want. You think being your little snitch was enough? What was in it for me?"

"Dan kept you out of jail, that's what was in it for you. Nobody's gonna keep you out of jail now."

"You too, baby. You and your buddy here," Rikers said, nodding at me, "You're in as deep as I am and you fucking know it."

Nicole and I traded glances. It was hard to argue with the truth, so I didn't even try. I just followed Nicole into the van. It smelled of dope and stale booze and maybe a little desperation. Rikers climbed in after us and closed the door. Then he sat down across from us.

"Cozy, huh?" he said.

Yeah, except for the gun, I thought.

"Ready?" the blonde said.

"Roll, baby," Rikers replied.

"Where we going?" Nic said.

Rikers looked at me. "What's her address?"

I knew what he wanted. We were going back to where it all began. Back to Daphne and the ghosts of Donny and Roy, and Ernie and Janelle. We were all circling each other, the living and the dead, and each time around the game got more and more dangerous.

"It's the middle of the night, Rikers," I said. "Visiting hours are over."

Rikers scowled. He shoved the gun in my face. "What's her fucking address?"

"You mean Daphne?"

Rikers smiled. "That's where the money is, right?"

We rolled out of town under cover of darkness and headed across the Golden Gate Bridge to the pot of gold that Rikers expected to find at the end of the rainbow. But I didn't see a rainbow or a pot of gold. Just a trail of bodies leading to a crime scene on sale to the highest bidder.

Somewhere north of San Quentin, Loretta decided we needed a little road music. She turned on the car stereo and cranked the volume to ten. Heavy metal thunder roared out of the speakers. I never much liked heavy metal, just sounded like some guy had plugged in his guitar and started screaming.

Jazz was more my speed. The noise filling the van could never match its beauty or its depth. What made jazz profound? I could never explain it. I could only feel it every time I dropped a needle on a record. But as the music raged around us, I had to admit that its fury matched the rage I felt inside me as we hurtled through the night, trapped in a killer's windowless van.

Then Loretta began singing along, wailing over the music as she struggled to carry the tune. But there wasn't a tune. There was just the noise, and the sound of her voice howling over it like a banshee. I glanced at Rikers. He was smiling and nodding along to a beat that didn't exist. I wondered if he was going to join her. Maybe we could all join in, I thought. Maybe a singalong was just what we needed to bring us all together and make it through the night.

Suddenly, Nicole, who was sitting behind Loretta and hadn't said a word since we left the lot, kicked Loretta's seatback as hard as she could and shouted at the top of her lungs, "Turn that shit off!"

Her outburst startled everyone, especially Loretta, who wasn't wearing her seatbelt. Her hands flew off the wheel as the blow pitched her toward the windshield like a crash test dummy. The van swerved, tires screeching, as it lurched across the lanes. I could hear the sounds of horns honking, and wondered how long it would be before we slammed head-on into oncoming traffic.

The gun fell out of Rikers's hands as the three of us were tossed from side to side in the back of the van. Nicole and I exchanged split-second glances, then dove for the gun. Rikers caught on fast and we all scrambled to find the gun, which was somewhere on the floor and impossible to see in the dark. Then the three of us found it at the same time, felt the cold steel in our hands, waved it above our heads as we struggled to grab hold of it.

Then the gun went off.

I looked up and saw Loretta slumped against the steering wheel. Blood spattered the windshield. This is how it ends, I thought, killed in a car crash with a heavy metal soundtrack.

Then the van lifted off the blacktop and somersaulted down the freeway. Last thing I remember.

****

We never did make it to Daphne's house that night. Some of us never made it at all. Loretta took a stray bullet just before the van went airborne and then Rikers did a swan dive into the center divider. Nicole and I somehow made it out alive, though even now, three weeks later, I still had no idea how we survived. The day I came to I still wasn't sure if I was dead or alive. Especially when I started having PTSD flashbacks of the crash.

I guess we were just lucky, if you could call being in a car crash lucky. We'd both been recuperating at home since we were released from the hospital. I was back on the obits beat and things were starting to feel almost normal, at least when it came to writing on deadline about the recently departed.

It was harder for Nicole to work from home, though. And not just because of her injuries. Crime reporters needed to be at the scene of the crime to get the story. But the fact of the matter was she'd been living in a crime scene ever since I dragged her into this mess.

But I'm getting ahead of myself. Nic and I were out of danger, but that didn't mean we were out of trouble. I found that out the hard way when the visitors began showing up while were still in the hospital. I'd heard stories about how it cheered people up to get visitors when they were laid up. I didn't have much firsthand experience to decide whether or not that was true. I tried to avoid hospitals. They always made me feel like I was coming down with something.

Maybe it was an occupational hazard, or maybe I was just superstitious. When you wrote about dead people for a living, you couldn't help thinking that before they died they were usually in a hospital. It was like the hospital was life's last stop, and it scared the hell out of me. And yet, here I was, in a hospital, having had what they like to call a brush with death. I wondered if the visitors were more of the same.

First up was Dan Bellamy, SFPD homicide cop and Nicole's married ex. Nicole and I were still in wheelchairs when Bellamy interviewed us in the hospital cafeteria. It was early and the air was filled with the smell of coffee and donuts. We hadn't had much time to get our stories straight. All we knew for sure was that the last thing we wanted to do was tell him the truth. But I felt awkward being with Nic and Bellamy. I knew they weren't on a date, but I still felt as if I was intruding. Then again, maybe I just didn't want to be there at all.

"So how you guys doing?" Bellamy said. "Feeling better?"

Nicole and I exchanged glances. I knew what he meant, but the fact of the matter was you never felt better when you were being interviewed by a cop. Especially when you had so much to hide.

"Yeah, better for sure," I said. "Still pretty sore though."

Bellamy nodded. "I'll bet," he said. Then he turned to Nicole. "How about you, Nic? You doing okay?"

Nicole offered a tight smile. I knew she wasn't happy having to sit for an interview with Bellamy, and it had nothing to do with the case.

"Umm hmm," she said, and left it at that.

"So I just wanted to go over what happened, if that's okay with you," Bellamy said, his eyes darting from me to Nic and back again.

"Sure, no problem," I said.

"So let's take it from the top," Bellamy said. "What were you guys doing out there with Rikers?"

Nicole and I traded glances, then Nic said, "He said he had a tip for me."

"What was the tip?"

"I don't know. He never told me."

Bellamy looked at me. "What were you doing there?

Crime's not your beat, right?"

Before I had a chance to answer, Nicole said, "We were hanging out when Rikers called."

"So you just went along for the ride?" Bellamy said.

I nodded. "Something like that."

"What about the guns?" Bellamy said.

"What about them?"

"Did you know that Rikers and the woman…" Bellamy paused to consult his notes, then looked up at us. "Loretta Holt. Did you know Rikers and Holt were armed?"

Nic and I traded glances, then we both shook our heads.

"So they were armed and you were in the van. Why'd you get in the van?"

"Rikers said he wanted to show us something."

"Did you know they were armed when you got in the van?"

"No."

"We recovered two guns at the scene of the accident. We're waiting for forensics to tell us which one was used to shoot Holt. Unless of course you want to tell me."

Nicole and I traded glances, but said nothing.

"Something's not adding up here, guys. She didn't shoot herself, right? Which means one of you shot her. Was that when the van crashed? When the gun went off?"

Nicole paused, then said, "Could we have a moment alone, Dan? Just the two of us?"

Bellamy looked up at Nicole with a surprised expression on his face. "Sure, I don't see why not," he said. Then he turned to me. "You need me to call a nurse?"

I shook my head. "I can manage, thanks," I said, and wheeled myself out of the cafeteria.

An hour later, Nicole wheeled into my room. I was in bed watching reruns. I muted the sound, then looked up at her.

"So what was that all about?" I said.

"It was about saving our asses."

I waited for the rest of it.

"I told him he needed to keep us out of it."

"He's a cop, Nic. Why would he do that?"

"Because he doesn't want his wife to know about us."

I stared at her, stunned by the news and impressed by her nerve.

"You're blackmailing him?"

Nicole gave a casual shrug. "Yeah, I guess I am. You got a problem with that?"

I shook my head. She had made her move knowing full well that Bellamy could have taken her down for blackmail and obstruction of justice.

"I can't believe you did that for us. What if he'd called your bluff?"

Nicole shrugged. "I guess they'd be wheeling us off to jail."

"How'd he take it?"

"Never saw it coming."

"I guess I should say thanks."

"Yeah, you should, seeing as how you got us into this mess."

I nodded. "Yeah, I did."

Nicole's eyes fell on the woody fridge magnet I'd found on the floor at Daphne's house. It was on the tray next to my bed. I'd been carrying it around in my pocket and had forgotten all about it until the nurses found it when they undressed me after the accident.

"What's this?" she said, picking up the magnet and examining it. "You collecting fridge magnets now?"

"I found it at Daphne's house."

"So? What are you doing with it?"

I shrugged. "I don't know yet."

"What are you gonna do about her?"

"Daphne?"

Nicole nodded. "Have you heard from her?"

I shook my head. "I keep dreaming I'm gonna wake up and she won't be the first thing I think of."

"But the rest of it is finished, right? I mean, everybody's dead, Dan's gonna keep us out of it...we can go back to work like it never happened."

"It's not that simple, Nic."

"Why? Because of her?"

"Her and the money."

"You mean the Paycheck Today heist?"

I nodded.

"Seriously, Max? You want to get killed along with everybody else who's after the money? The bodies are piling up, in case you didn't notice."

"It's not that simple, Nic."

"You know what's simple? Staying alive. Buy a lottery ticket instead. You'll have better luck."

"I wish I could, but they won't let me forget it."

A worried look shadowed Nicole's face. "Who's they?"

I thought of Benny and Ida Velasco, and his posse of grateful parolees. "I'm out on bail, Nic."

"I don't understand, what are you talking about?"

"The less you know, the better."

Nicole's face tightened with annoyance. "What? You're not gonna tell me?"

"You're in the clear now, Nic."

"And you're not?"

I shook my head. "Not yet."

Chapter 19

They let me go the next morning. I was happy to get out of the hospital, but the truth was I felt safer as a patient. It was as if the hospital could protect me from what I knew was waiting for me once I got outside. The doctors had patched me up and now they were sending me back into the world. But from what I knew of the world it might not be long before I was back for more patching up. Unless of course I found myself added to the pile of bodies that had grown since the day I met Daphne Swan.

I had just finished changing into my street clothes when a black orderly with a Black Panthers afro rolled a wheelchair into my room.

"Are we ready to go home, Mr. McQuinn?" the orderly said.

I nodded. "Yeah, I'm ready."

"I heard that. Everybody's ready when it's time to go home. You got a ride, right?"

"Ride share," I said.

Nic was discharged before me, and the thought had crossed my mind that maybe she could pick me up. But I'd put her through enough already, and when she didn't offer I figured she wanted some time away to get her life as close back to normal as possible. I hoped I hadn't lost her, and I knew that I would miss her if I did.

The orderly made a face. "You got nobody picking

you up? Man, that ain't right."

"It's okay," I said. "I'm just happy to be going home."

"All right, then," the orderly said, "let's roll."

I settled into the wheelchair.

"Fasten your seatbelt," the orderly grinned.

He was about to wheel me out of the room when an unexpected visitor appeared in the doorway.

"Hey, Max, how you doing?" Benny Velasco said.

I was worried about what might happen when I left the hospital. But the fact of the matter was I didn't have to walk out of the hospital to run into trouble. I could just wait for it to walk into my room.

I looked up at Benny, which, given how big he was, was the only way you could look at him. You could never look down at a man like Benny Velasco, even if you were wearing elevator shoes with the button pushed to ten.

"Hey Benny," I said, surprised to see him, "what are you doing here?"

"I'm gonna take you home. You need a ride, right?"

I did need a ride, but how did Benny know, I wondered.

"He was gonna call a ride share," the orderly said.

Benny frowned and shook his head. "That's no way to go home from the hospital."

"That's what I told him."

"You need a friend to take you home," Benny said.

"Damn straight," the orderly said.

"I'll take it from here," Benny said, taking control of the wheelchair.

"You take care now," I heard the orderly say as Benny wheeled me out of the room.

His words echoed in my ears as we rolled down the

corridor toward the entrance. If I was supposed to take care, what was I doing with Benny Velasco?

A supersized SUV was parked at the curb. It seemed to take up the entire block. I never understood why people wanted to drive giant SUVs, but I could see why Benny wanted one. A supersized guy needed a supersized ride. He'd never be able to squeeze into anything else.

Ida was sitting up front in the passenger seat. She waited until we got closer, then rolled down the window, looked at me, and smiled.

"Hi Max, feeling better?"

I was until you and Benny showed up, I wanted to say. Instead I just smiled back at her and said, "Yeah, much better, thanks."

"Here you go," Benny said as he opened a door. "Plenty of room back here."

I nodded and climbed into the back seat.

Benny went around to the driver's side and climbed in behind the wheel. He looked over at Ida and smiled.

"Ready, pumpkin?"

Ida smiled back at him. "Sure am, hon."

Benny glanced in the rearview. "How about you, Max? You ready?"

I was ready to go home, I thought. Was there something else I should be ready for?

"Yeah, sure," I said, not knowing what else to say.

"That's what I like to hear," Benny, and turned the key. The car rumbled to life and Benny pulled away from the curb.

"How'd you know I was getting out today, Benny?" I said.

"I make it my business to know, Max," Benny said.

I nodded. No sense in pushing it.

"I'll tell you what else he knows," Ida said.

I looked up at her and waited for the rest of it.

"The bitch doesn't know we're coming."

"Excuse me," I said, as dread tied a knot in the pit of my stomach.

Benny glanced in the rearview. "Forgot to tell you, we're making a little side trip before we take you home. You don't mind, do you?"

"Where exactly are we going, Benny?"

Benny and Ida exchanged glances.

"Should we tell him?" Ida said.

"Sure, pumpkin."

Ida turned around and looked at me. "We're gonna go get the money that belongs to us."

"Money?" I said. I could feel myself starting to sweat. I had a feeling I knew where this was going, and I'd been there before.

"I got it coming," Ida said.

"We're going to Daphne's house?" I said.

"Yeah, and she don't know it," Benny said.

"That's crazy, Benny. What, you think she's got it in the house?"

Ida's face hardened. "I don't care if we have to tear the fuckin' place apart. We're gonna get it."

"Hold on now, pumpkin," Benny said. "Don't get yourself all worked up. She ain't gonna put up a fight."

That's what you think, I thought. I took a deep breath and looked out the window as we headed toward the Golden Gate Bridge.

The wreckage of the van had been towed away, along with whatever was left of Rikers and Loretta, but the skid marks and scorched shoulder were still there, like some weird memorial. I flashed on the moment the van went airborne, and wondered how Nic and I survived. We walked away with more than a scratch, but we walked away. Why did I survive, I wondered. Was it so I could face more hell down the road that led to Daphne's house?

"Must've been a helluva ride," Benny said as we rolled past the scene of the accident. "So how'd you get hooked up with Rikers?"

He glanced at me in the rearview and from the look in his eyes I figured he saw the stunned expression on my face.

"You look surprised, Max," he said.

"Yeah, I guess I am. How'd you know about Rikers?"

"I'm a bail bondsman, Max. Bailed him out a bunch of times."

"Rikers was good for business, wasn't he, hon?" Ida said.

"Sure was, pumpkin. I love repeat offenders."

"But how'd you know about me and Rikers?"

"Word gets around, you know how it is."

I didn't know how it was, but I was catching on fast.

"He was after it, too, right? That's what you were doing when it happened, heading up to the house. If it wasn't for the crash, he might've beat us to it."

"Lucky for us, huh?" Ida chimed in.

I looked up at Ida and saw that was she was smiling. I felt a chill run through me. Rikers may have been a stone-cold killer who got what was coming to him, but Ida being happy about it so she could cash in made me feel sorry for the guy.

"What if she doesn't have the money?" I said.

"She's got it," Ida snapped.

"She told me she didn't know what happened to Archie's score."

"She's lying!" Ida said, her face hard as a rock.

I wondered if her hatred of Daphne went beyond the money, and had something to do with the fact they were both married to Archie Gibbs. Ida was there first, which I suppose gave her seniority. But Daphne was younger and prettier, and maybe that accounted for Ida's jealousy and rage. I dreaded what might happen when Benny and Ida barged in on her.

Daphne would also no doubt wonder what I was doing with them. What could I tell her besides the truth? That I was no better than all the other vultures circling around her? I hadn't heard from her while I was in the hospital, and I wondered if perhaps she'd heard about Rikers passing, and figured now that everybody was dead we were through as well. Maybe that was for the best, I told myself, hoping that I would believe it. But any addict could tell you the same story about how they were going to kick the habit.

"We're here," Benny said.

I looked out the window as Benny nosed the SUV into the driveway. I flashed on the day I met Daphne, fresh from a dip in the pool. It seemed so long ago now, but maybe that was because of all the blood that had flowed downstream. The "For Sale" sign was still planted in the lawn, but now it said "Sold." She'd pulled it off, I thought. Killed Roy and Donny, then sold the crime scene where they died. Not bad for a gangster's widow. Archie would have been proud. I wondered if the fact that she'd sold the house explained why I hadn't heard from her. Maybe now that she'd offloaded the house, she was busy making plans that didn't include a newspaper obituary writer.

Benny opened the glove compartment and took out a 9mm semiautomatic. He ejected the magazine, checked to see if it was loaded, then slid it back into the gun until it clicked.

"Let's go," he said. He climbed out of the car and shoved the gun in his waistband.

"Yeah, let's go," Ida said, itching for a fight.

I stepped in front of Benny and Ida and held up my hand. "Let me talk to her first, okay? Tell her what's going on. Before we all barge in on her."

Benny and Ida traded glances. Benny tightened his grip on the gun.

"I don't like it," Ida said, a suspicious look in her eyes.

"You got five minutes," Benny said. "Then we're comin' in."

I nodded and headed toward the front door. Daphne must have seen me coming because the front door flew open before I got there. She wore a black halter top and cutoffs, the kind of outfit that made her look good coming or going. She stared at me as a surprised look swept across her face.

"Max…?"

I nodded. "Yeah, Max."

She spotted the bruises on my face. "What happened to your face?"

"Rikers is dead."

Her eyes went wide. "Rikers is dead? How? What happened?"

"Never mind that now."

She looked past me and saw Benny and Ida. "What's

going on? What are you doing here?"

"Can we talk inside?" I said.

"Yeah, sure," she said, and stepped aside.

I walked into the house. Stacks of moving boxes filled the living room. Rolled-up rugs lay on the floor. I noticed that the walls were bare of artworks. Daphne wasn't wasting any time. I wondered if she even planned to say goodbye. Then I wondered if the ghosts would be moving with her.

"Going somewhere?" I said.

"Yeah, I sold the house so I have to move."

I nodded. "I saw it said the house was pending. Congratulations."

"I'm sorry I haven't been in touch. I've just been so busy with selling the house and packing up, you know how it is."

"Yeah, I know how it is," I said. I was learning fast how it was, and didn't like the way it felt. "So where you going?"

"I'm putting everything in storage and checking in at the Fairmont. I always did want to live in the city."

"Yeah, I remember you telling me that."

I could feel her slipping away from me. Maybe because everybody who was in the way was dead. She didn't need me to save her anymore.

"You said Rikers is dead…"

"Yeah, so you don't have to worry about him anymore. Mick and Janis are dead too."

"Did they kill him?"

"They tried."

"Are you going to tell me what happened?"

I shook my head. "It's a long story and we don't have the time."

"What's going on? Who's out there? Is that Ida, Archie's ex?"

I nodded.

"Who's the guy with her?"

"Her husband, Benny Velasco. Runs a bail bonds business south of Market." I left out the part about how we both might need a bail bondsman sooner rather than later.

"What do they want?"

"Archie's score."

Daphne's eyes widened. "Archie's score? I don't know anything about that."

"I guess they think you do."

She moved closer to me. "Max, I'm scared."

I didn't believe her, but I liked the way she moved into my arms, so I let it ride.

"Hold me."

I held her close, and when she looked up at me, I kissed her. I wondered if it was the last good kiss, and I wanted it to last forever.

****

But just then the door flew open.

"See, I told you he was fucking her." Ida said as she stood in the doorway.

Daphne looked at her and her face darkened. "What are you doing here?"

Ida's face hardened. She grabbed the gun out of Benny's waistband and levelled it at Daphne at point-blank range.

"The money, bitch! That's what I'm doing here! Where the fuck is it?"

Daphne stayed close to me, her eyes on the gun.

"Hold on now, pumpkin," Benny said, apparently

alarmed by Ida's move.

Ida glanced at him and shook her head. I had no idea what she was going to do next, and I didn't think she knew either. What I did know was that I was way over having people point guns at me.

"Let's just take it slow, okay?" Benny said, reaching for the gun.

Ida glanced at him, then let him disarm her. A shadow of disappointment fell across her face. She'd lost her chance to shoot somebody. I wondered if she'd ever pulled the trigger, seen a bullet tear the life out of a living thing, or if the gun was just a prop.

Benny looked around at the moving boxes. "Guess you're gonna take the money and run, huh?"

"What money?"

"Don't play dumb, Daphne," Benny said.

"Archie's score. Where is it?" Ida said.

Daphne sneered. "Seriously? That's why you're here?"

"Yeah, that's why we're here. So where is it?" Ida said.

"There is no money, you stupid bitch, and if there is I don't know where it is, okay?" Daphne said. "Archie never told me. You want to know where it is, go ask him. Maybe he'll rise up out of the grave and tell you."

The room fell silent. Daphne and I traded glances. Benny and Ida did likewise.

"She's lying," Ida said.

"She's telling the truth," I said. "She doesn't know anything about it."

Ida scowled. "You're in it together, the two of you, aren't you?"

Daphne glanced at me. We were in something

together, Ida had that part right. But it had nothing to do with Archie's score. It would have been easier if it was about the money. Instead it was about a coverup soaked through with blood and desire.

"You got it wrong, Ida," I said. "It's not about the money. If it was we'd be long gone by now. You're chasing something that doesn't exist."

"Like hell we are," Benny said. He nodded at Daphne. "She's holding out on us, maybe you are too."

"He's fucking you, isn't he?" Ida said.

"What if he is?" Daphne said. "Beats fucking a hag like you."

Ida's face twisted with shock and anger. But I swore I could see her eyes welling up.

Benny glared at Daphne. "What did you say?"

"You heard me," Daphne said. "You want me to say it again?"

Benny raised the gun and pointed it at Daphne. "Nobody's gonna want to fuck you when you're dead," he said.

"Do it!" Ida said, her voice trembling with rage. "Do it!"

Suddenly, without waiting for Benny to pull the trigger, Ida lunged at Daphne. She grabbed her by the hair and yanked it hard, as if she was trying to pull it out of her head. Daphne screamed and clawed Ida's face. Blood streaked down Ida's cheek as she and Daphne fell to the floor.

Benny and I traded glances as Daphne and Ida tore into each other. They slammed into a stack of boxes, toppling the one on top. It burst open as it fell to the floor and woody memorabilia spilled out. I thought of Archie and wondered what he would think if could see his ex-wives tangled in a catfight on the living room floor. Their clothes were torn and both of them were bleeding from clawing each other. Then Ida rolled on top of Daphne and tried to strangle her.

Benny scowled. "God damn it, Ida! Stop it!"

He shoved the gun into his waistband, then bent down and tried to pull Ida away from Daphne. But Ida wouldn't listen. Daphne gasped for air as Ida's hands tightened around her neck. Benny and I traded glances, then both of us bent down and grabbed Ida. She snarled like a wild animal as we pulled her off of Daphne.

Then we heard a hard knock on the door and I knew the show was over.

"Police! Open up!" said a voice I'd heard before.

Chapter 20

Everybody froze. Traded glances. Looked around the room, as if there might be a place to hide. Then Ida remembered the gun tucked into Benny's waistband.

"Benny, the gun!" she said.

She tried to grab it just as Benny reached for it. They were both fumbling with it when the door burst open. Bellamy and Robinson stepped inside just as the gun fell on the floor.

"Gun!" Robinson said.

Bellamy and Robinson pulled their guns. Our hands shot into the air. Robinson glanced at Daphne and Ida.

"What do we got here, the gorgeous ladies of wrestling?"

Daphne and Ida's faces reddened with embarrassment.

"She started it," Daphne said, sounding like she was in junior high.

Ida glared at her. "Yeah, and I would've finished it too, bitch!"

"You wish," Daphne sneered. "I still can't believe Archie married you. He must've been drunk or something."

Ida's eyes went hot with rage. She lunged at Daphne, but Benny grabbed her and pulled her back next to him.

"That's enough, girls," Robinson said.

Bellamy nodded at the gun. "Slide it over to me. Nice and easy."

Benny slid the gun over to Bellamy.

"Who are you?"

"Benny Velasco, Scot Free Bail Bonds. Maybe you heard of me."

"Yeah, we heard of you," Robinson said. "We take the bad guys off the street and you put 'em right back there."

Bellamy glanced at the gun. "You got a permit to carry?"

"Yeah, I do, as a matter of fact," Benny said.

"It expired," Ida said.

Benny looked at her with a stunned expression. "You were supposed to renew it."

"I forgot."

"You forgot? What the fuck do you mean, you forgot?"

"It means I forgot, okay?" Ida snapped. "I can't remember everything."

"What the fuck, Ida! I didn't ask you to remember everything. I just asked you to renew the permit."

"You know what? You can tell us all about it downtown," Bellamy said.

Benny looked sharply at Bellamy. "Downtown? What do you mean, downtown?"

"It means you're under arrest."

"On what charge?"

Bellamy nodded at the gun. "Carrying a concealed weapon without a permit."

"I got a permit!"

Bellamy turned to Robinson. "Get 'em out of here."

Robinson cuffed Benny, then turned to Ida, who

started crying at the sight of the cuffs.

"Oh, for Christ's sake, Ida," Benny said, annoyed and embarrassed.

"Let's go, kids," Robinson said as she led Benny and Ida to the door.

"This ain't over!" Benny shouted over his shoulder. "I'll be back!"

Bellamy shook his head wearily, then looked at me. "Good to see you up and around, McQuinn. But I gotta say, trouble just seems to follow you around, doesn't it?" He turned to Daphne. "We haven't met. Detective Dan Bellamy, Homicide, San Francisco Police Department," he said, flashing his badge.

Daphne stiffened. I wondered if she felt the ghosts of Roy and Donny passing through. I know I did.

"What do you want with me?" Daphne said.

"I'm trying to solve a puzzle, Ms. Swan."

"I don't like puzzles."

"Neither do I, but I have to figure 'em out anyway. So maybe you can help me figure out how a gun registered to your husband was used in an attempted murder."

Daphne stared at Bellamy. "Murder?"

"*Attempted* murder," Bellamy said. "But we'll give 'em an A for effort."

I could see the color drain out of Daphne's face.

"Back to the gun," Bellamy said. "Did your husband have any weapons on the premises?"

"Yeah, I guess so. I never saw them. Guns scare me."

I tried not to smile. She was good. If I'd had an Oscar in my pocket I would've pulled it out and given it to her. I flashed on the day she drew down on Mick and

Janis while we were sitting by the pool. She didn't look scared. She looked ready. Maybe she was born ready.

"Any idea how his gun ended up at a crime scene?"

Daphne shrugged and shook her head. "Sorry."

Bellamy nodded, then looked around at the moving boxes. "Moving out, huh?"

"Yeah, I sold the house."

"I wouldn't go far if I were you, Ms. Swan. We may have more questions." Bellamy turned to me. "So what are you doing here, McQuinn?"

Before I could answer, Daphne jumped in and said, "We met when he wrote Archie's obituary."

"Grief counselor too now, huh?"

I said nothing. Bellamy looked at Daphne. "By the way, you want to tell me about the catfight?"

"They think I know something about Archie's last job."

"The Paycheck Today job?"

Daphne nodded.

"Do you?"

"No, I don't, but nobody seems to believe me."

"Right," Bellamy said, like he didn't believe her either. "That'll do it for today. We'll be in touch." Then he turned and walked out of the house.

A moment later, the door opened.

"Almost forgot," Bellamy said, standing in the doorway. "We'll let you know if forensics lifts any prints off the gun." He offered a cold smile. "Hope they're not yours."

Then he walked out again.

"What if they find my prints on the gun?" Daphne said, her face tense with worry.

"They won't," I said, remembering what Nic had

told me about how difficult it was to lift prints from a gun's oily surface.

Daphne looked up at me. Her face was scratched and streaked with blood, which somehow made her even more beautiful.

"You sure?" she said.

I wasn't sure of anything anymore, but I nodded and said, "Yeah."

She moved into my arms. I wiped the blood away from her face with my bare hands.

"I'm a mess, aren't I?" she said.

I smiled. "Not a chance."

"I'll be right back," she said, moving out of my arms. "I just want to clean up."

"You sure you don't want to go to the ER? Some of those scratches look pretty bad."

Daphne shook her head. "Nothing a little hydrogen peroxide won't cure," she said, and headed toward the bathroom.

I looked down at my hands. They were smeared with Daphne's blood. I thought about washing it off, but then it occurred to me that maybe I should leave it there to remind me of how much blood had been spilled since the day I met her.

I surveyed the room, which Daphne and Ida had turned into a shambles. Woody memorabilia was scattered across the floor. A photograph caught my eye. I bent down and picked it up. It was a snapshot of Archie and a voluptuous, middle-aged Latina woman with glossy black hair and dark eyes. They were standing in front of a woody convertible, which was parked in front of a place called La Bahia.

The car was a beauty and so was the woman. But

what really got my attention was her outfit. She wore a blood-red peasant blouse, a long black dress, and boots. But that was just for starters. Ammo belts filled with bullets crisscrossed her breasts and she wore pistols in holsters on her hips. She reminded me of the pictures I'd seen in a magazine of the female soldiers, or *soldaderas*, who fought with Pancho Villa and Emilio Zapata in the Mexican Revolution. But the shooting stopped a hundred years ago. Who was she fighting now?

I was still looking at the photo when Daphne came up to me. She'd changed her clothes and washed her face, but the scratches were still there, and I wondered if they would leave scars from a war that was far from over.

"What's that?" she said.

"It fell out of the box," I said, nodding at the memorabilia on the floor. "Who's the woman?"

Daphne smiled. "That's Lola Santos. We used to catch her shows at a Latin club called La Bahia."

"Didn't know you were into that kind of music."

"Archie was into it. I just went along for the drinks. Then it turned out that he and Lola both had woodies so they used to hang out."

"Was it more than that?" I said, looking at the photo.

Daphne shrugged. "What if it was? Does it matter now?"

"What's gonna happen to Archie's car?"

Daphne shrugged like she didn't care. "Some classic car dealer wants to buy it."

"Woody Wonders?"

Daphne's face lit up with surprise. "Yeah, how'd you know?"

"Just a lucky guess," I said, remembering the fridge magnet I found on the floor in the kitchen. "So where's

Woody Wonders?"

"Someplace in the East Bay. Why?"

"I'd like to see Archie's woody." I glanced at the photo. "Funny outfit, huh?"

"Santos?"

"Yeah."

Daphne chuckled. "Archie knew all kinds of people."

She was right about that. And now all kinds of people were crawling out of the woodwork looking for the loot that Archie had stashed away somewhere. Was Archie's *soldadera* one of them? I realized I wanted to know if she was. Maybe it was the car or maybe it was the outfit.

Then my cellphone rang. I reached for it and saw it was Nicole. I had promised to call her when I got out of the hospital, but then Benny showed up and I forgot all about it. But now was not the time. I slipped the phone back into my pocket and let Nic go to voicemail.

Daphne looked up at me. "Do you have to go?" she said.

"Not yet." I looked around the room. "So when are the movers coming?"

"First thing tomorrow morning." She paused, then said, "Can you stay until then? I don't want to be alone."

I don't want to be alone.

That was what Daphne told me the night she gunned down Roy and Donny. But the truth was I didn't want to be alone either.

Daphne looked around at the moving boxes with a kind of longing, as if they were filled with the life she had shared with Archie.

"It hurts to be alone, doesn't it?" she said.

195

I looked at her. I knew she was in my head, but could she also read my mind?

"I guess I'm used to it," I said with a shrug.

Daphne gave a sad smile. "Which part—the hurting or the loneliness?"

I gave myself some time to think about it. Then again, I'd thought about it all my life, and still didn't have an answer.

"Where we going with this, Daphne?"

She gave me a quizzical look. "With what? Us?"

"With everything."

"That's a big question, Max."

"Is it?"

"Well, yeah, I mean, look at everything we've been through—"

"Like murder, for example?" I said.

Daphne stiffened. "It was self-defense."

"Whatever, they're dead and we covered it up."

"They would've killed me, Max, okay? Are we going to go through all this again? "Why didn't you turn me in—"

I cut her off with a kiss. It was the only answer I could think of, and the only one that was true.

She looked up at me and smiled. "I guess that was why, huh?"

I said nothing, just held her tight like a man who could feel a woman slipping away from him.

"I couldn't have done any of this without you," she said.

I nodded, but I worried that now that she'd done it, she could do the rest without me.

She must have read the look in my eyes, because she said, "Don't worry so much, everything's gonna be fine."

"Why? Because we got away with it?"

Daphne shrugged. "Well, we did get away with it, didn't we? I mean, they all killed each other off. We were so worried about Rikers and look what happened. Now there's nobody left to worry about."

Hours later I woke up in the middle of the night. Daphne lay asleep beside me, breathing softly into her pillow. I climbed out of bed and went into the bathroom to take a piss. I looked out the window into the dark and that was when I saw them. Roy and Donny were crawling across the front lawn toward the street. But they never got there because the ground kept opening up in front of them like a grave and they kept falling into it.

"So how come you write about dead people?" Daphne had asked me before she turned the lights out.

Because that's what I see, I thought, as I looked out the window. You never get away with anything. I flushed the toilet and crawled back into bed next to Daphne. She turned into me as I pulled up the comforter. I could feel her warmth course through me as I lay awake until dawn.

****

Two hours later Daphne dropped me off at the San Rafael Transit Center so I could catch a bus into the city. She leaned across the seat and kissed me like she was a wife sending her husband off to work in San Francisco. It wasn't like that, of course. I just wasn't sure what it was. She promised to call me once she'd checked in at the Fairmont. But she told me it might be later in the day because she had to wait for the movers, etc. It was then that I jumped headfirst off the cliff and asked her to stay with me instead of at the Fairmont. Daphne's eyes widened with surprise. I knew it was the last thing she expected me to say. Hell, it was the last thing I expected to say.

Then she smiled and shook her head. "Let's not ruin it, Max."

"Ruin what?" I said.

She glanced out the windshield at the bus. Passengers were climbing aboard.

"You're gonna miss your bus."

The hour's ride gave me plenty of time to think, which was probably the last thing I wanted to do. The whole idea was crazy and I knew it. What did we share besides murder and a coverup? And yet, wasn't that enough? The truth was that now that Rikers was dead and the house was sold, Daphne was free. Free to do to anything. Free to go anywhere. Free to forget about me. And maybe that was what I was afraid of. Freedom. I wondered how many guys had agreed to play house just because they were afraid of losing their girlfriends. But Daphne wasn't my girlfriend. It would have been easier if she was. Instead, she was the woman for whom I would do anything.

Chapter 21

I called Nicole from the cab on the ride home from the bus station.

"I've been calling you."

"I know."

"Why didn't you call me back?"

Then, before I could reply, Nic said, "Never mind. You were with her, right?"

"It's a long story."

"As usual. You okay?"

"Yeah, I'm okay."

"You sure?"

I smiled to myself. Good question. Nic. "No."

"That's what I figured. Text me later, I'm on deadline."

The cab pulled up in front of my building. Cornell, the manager, was out front hosing down the sidewalk. He turned off the water and looked at me as I stepped out of the cab. Cornell was a stocky black guy in his fifties who'd been a bus driver for twenty-five years. But driving a bus wasn't the only thing he'd done. He'd also played the market from day one, and when he was ready, he retired and bought an apartment building. I never quite understood why he would want to invest in the hassle of running an apartment building, but Cornell didn't seem to mind. I figured that maybe owning a building and deciding who lived there made him feel like some kind of king. Cornell also dug jazz as much as I did, which meant we got along fine.

"Hey Max," he said.

"Hey Cornell."

"How you doing?" he said as he checked out the bruises on my face.

"I'm doing, Cornell, you know what I'm saying?"

Cornell nodded. "I hear you, brother."

"I'll catch you later, man. I gotta get to work."

I was about to walk into the building when Cornell said, "You got some company while you were gone."

I stopped and turned to him as my stomach tightened. He had turned the water back on and resumed hosing down the sidewalk.

"What kind of company?"

"Guy and a girl, came by last night."

"You get their names?"

Cornell shook his head as he waved the nozzle across the patch of concrete in front of the building.

"Didn't ask."

"They say what they wanted?"

"Nope. But the dude had an accent."

"Accent?" I searched my mind for anyone I knew who spoke with an accent but came up empty.

Cornell nodded.

"What kind of accent?"

Cornell shrugged. "It was an accent, man, like he ain't from here, you know what I'm sayin'?"

"Thanks for letting me know."

Cornell nodded and I went into the building. I didn't like unexpected guests, especially now, when so much of what was happening in my life was unexpected. I pushed the button for the elevator, then decided to take the stairs.

I wasn't sure why, exactly. Maybe I just needed to keep moving.

I reached the third floor and headed to my apartment. The muffled sounds of conversations, TV shows, and music accompanied me as I walked down the corridor. The smell of coffee, breakfast on the table, seeped through the walls. People still alive, I thought, as I unlocked the door to my apartment and went inside.

I paused for a moment before turning on the lights, as if expecting to find another surprise waiting for me. But all I found was a chilly apartment that seemed colder than usual. I went into the kitchen and put on a pot of coffee, then switched on my laptop. As I scrolled through my emails, I noticed that the Ripper had sent me a zip file, which I assumed contained background materials on the day's obits.

Just then my cellphone rang.

"I heard you're out of the hospital."

"Yeah, just got out yesterday."

"Congratulations. Ready to go back to work?"

"Can't wait," I said.

"Lovely. I sent you a zip file, not sure if you saw it."

"Yeah, it's on my desktop. Haven't opened it yet."

"I expect we're back in business then."

"Yeah, we're good."

"By the way, if you don't mind me asking, what the bloody hell happened to you guys? What were you and Nicole doing out there in the middle of the night anyway?"

I paused as the van somersaulted through my mind. "We were chasing a lead."

Dickie scoffed. "Some lead," he said, and ended the call.

I poured myself a cup of coffee, then sat down in front of my computer and began downloading the dead.

First up was an ex-porn star who had renounced her wicked ways and joined a convent. She took a vow of silence and died forty years later without having said a word. I wondered how hard it must have been for her to keep her mouth shut for all that time.

She was followed by the star of a hit seventies show about a spy with a girl in every port. He came out as gay after the show went off the air, proving once again that no matter what you thought you were seeing, the truth was something else.

Then came one of those guys who risked his life during World War II to save his buddies as the enemy strafed him with machine gun fire. I figured that was why they called it the greatest generation.

They all shuffled past my desk on their way to the grave, and as the day passed from morning to afternoon and the shadows lengthened across my living room, I realized I was shuffling along with them. They were ahead of me, but we were all heading in the same direction. Life on the obituaries desk reminded me of my own mortality on a daily basis. Though I had to say that lately I was being reminded of it a little too often.

I filed my copy around eight that night, then called Nicole and asked her if she was up for a night out.

"A night out where?"

"A club in East Oakland."

"East Oakland? Are you kidding me?"

"So is that a no?"

"No offense," Nicole said, "but the last time I went out with you I ended up in the hospital."

I got to *La Bahia* a little after ten. The club was on

International Boulevard in Oakland, in the heart of what homicide cops liked to call the shooting galleries south of the interstate. The lot was crowded with lowriders, pickup trucks, and SUVs, and I had to circle it a couple of times before I found a space in the back. I killed the engine, then looked up at the blazing neon marquee:

Live Onstage! Lola Santos, La Soldadera!

I had no idea who she was, but I figured she was some kind of star. I got out of the car and headed toward the club. The woody convertible I'd seen in the photo at Daphne's house was parked near the entrance, under the watchful eye of a uniformed security guard.

"Nice car," I said, admiring the convertible, which appeared to be in original condition.

"It's hers," the uniformed security guard said, nodding at the life-size cutout of Lola Santos by the door.

I recognized her as the woman in the photo. Santos was a voluptuous, middle-aged Latina woman with glossy black hair and dark eyes. She wore a colorful peasant blouse and a long black dress. Ammo belts were slung across her breasts and she wore pistols in holsters on her hips. Just like in the photo.

She reminded me of the pictures I'd seen in the *Bugle*'s morgue of the female soldiers, or *soldaderas*, who fought with Pancho Villa and Emilio Zapata in the Mexican Revolution. The fighting may have ended a hundred years ago, but the look was just getting started. Now it was part of Santos's act, just as it was for the kids I saw on the street wearing camouflage and combat boots. They'd never seen a battlefield or faced enemy fire, but they liked the style, if not the blood and bullets.

I opened the door and salsa music rushed out into the parking lot. The guard gave me a sidelong glance as

I stepped into the club, as if to determine whether or not I might be trouble. I stood by the door and looked around. Cocktail tables filled with fans waiting for the show to start dotted the room. Cute young barmaids in tank tops and cleavage balanced trays filled with drinks as they made their way through the room. I could hear the roar of conversation, the tinkle of glasses. A Latina singer on the sound system, whom I assumed was Lola Santos, rode the energy in the room.

A stocky Mexican doorman rocking a mustache and a burgundy tuxedo came up to me.

"Welcome to Bahia, *señor*. You have a reservation?"

Just then, a spotlight lit up the stage, and the crowd erupted in cheers, wolf whistles, and applause. A group of musicians, presumably *La Soldadera*'s band, took the stage. I turned to the doorman.

"No reservation," I said, "just thought I'd stop by and catch the show."

The doorman offered an apologetic smile. "I'm sorry, *señor*, but there are no tables available. *La Soldadera*, she is very popular."

I looked around the club, then spotted an empty stool at the bar.

"Mind if I sit at the bar?"

The doorman nodded. "*Si, señor*." He extended his arm in the direction of the bar. "Enjoy the show."

"Thanks," I said, and headed over to the bar.

I slid onto the stool and waited for the bartender. I didn't have to wait long.

"What can I get you, my friend?" he said with a sly smile, like he knew more than I did. He wore a Mexican bandit's mustache and a slick black pompadour, and looked as if he would fit right in with Santos' posse.

I made it easy for him and ordered a beer.

"Your first time at La Bahia?" he said as he opened the bottle.

"How'd you know?" I said as he set the bottle and a half-filled glass in front of me.

The bartender shrugged. "*Hombre*, you're alone. Nobody comes to La Bahia alone. You need a woman on your arm. La Bahia is for lovers."

"Thanks for the advice," I said, and sipped my beer.

The bartender nodded and moved away. I flashed on Daphne, and realized I hadn't heard from her since she dropped me off at the bus terminal. Was it too late to call her and tell her I wished she was with me? Like the man said, La Bahia was for lovers. I checked my watch, then reached for my cellphone. I tried her cell first, but got voicemail. Then I made the mistake of calling the Fairmont. Because that was when I learned that no one by the name of Daphne Swan was registered at the hotel.

Moments later, an MC in a sparkly dinner jacket bounded onto the stage and grabbed the microphone.

"Good evening, ladies and gentlemen, welcome to Bahia. Please give a warm welcome to the great Lola Santos, *La Soldadera*!"

There was another round of applause, then the band started playing. Moments later, Santos emerged from the wings. The audience roared as she swaggered across the stage. She gave a warm smile, then moved to the microphone and began singing a romantic mariachi ballad.

The audience quieted down as her sultry voice took over the room. Couples were slipping into each other's arms and slow dancing to the song. Suddenly, I wanted to dance, wanted Daphne in my arms. But instead all I could do was let the song wash over me. The lyrics were in Spanish, but I didn't need to speak the language to understand it. The music told me what the lyrics meant, and so did the ache in my heart. Where was she, I wondered, if she wasn't at the Fairmont? Out there somewhere, without me. What did I expect? That we would live happily ever after? I knew she wasn't that kind of woman. Trouble was, I wanted her anyway.

The guard glanced at me again when I emerged from the club, and I wondered if he checked out everybody twice, just to make sure nobody sneaked past him. Being a security guard was boring duty, and standing outside a club night after night wearing a uniform that never quite seemed to fit while everybody else was inside having fun had to weigh on a man.

I nodded at the guard, who returned the favor, then paused to check out the woody, which was still parked by the entrance. It glistened in the evening mist that had settled on the car, and looked like a dream from another time, which I guess it was. I waited until the guard had lost sight of me in the crush of fans emerging from the club and walking to their cars. I looked around to get my bearings, then walked around the building until I found the stage door. Fans were gathering by the door, autograph pads in their hands, their faces filled with hope and anticipation. I checked my watch, then hung back in the shadows and waited for the door to open.

Twenty minutes later, Santos stepped out into the pool of light created by the lantern mounted above the door. She was still wearing the guns and ammo belts. I wondered if she slept with them, an angel of the revolution, ready at a moment's notice to take up the fight. The fans rushed toward her, thrusting their autograph pads. Santos smiled and began signing her autograph. I held back until the fans moved away clutching their autographs, then stepped forward. Santos was about to walk back inside. She gave a me a curious glance as I approached her.

"No autograph, *señor*?" she said.

I shook my head. "I'm a reporter for the *Bay Area Bugle*."

"A reporter?"

I nodded.

"Then you should talk to my press secretary, *señor*." She turned to walk back into the club.

"I'm not that kind of reporter, Ms. Santos."

She turned and looked at me. "What kind are you?"

"I write obituaries."

She offered a sly smile. "Then why would you want to talk to me? I'm still alive, no?"

"I'd like to talk to you about Archie Gibbs."

****

I met her in the bar after hours. She chose a table and we ordered a round of drinks. I looked around at the sea of empty tables dotted with white tablecloths. The show was over and the fans had all gone home. All that remained were the waiters and busboys and dishwashers cleaning up after them. The bartender who had informed me that no one came to La Bahia without a woman on his arm came up to the table carrying a tray. I noticed that there were three drinks on it. Santos looked up at him and smiled.

"*Gracias,* Ramon," she said.

"*De nada, mujer*," Ramon said as he set our drinks in front of us.

Then he surprised me by setting the third drink down on the table, pulling up a chair, and joining us. It was then that I understood that he was more than just the bartender.

"To *La Soldadera*!" Ramon said, raising his glass in a toast.

Santos lowered her eyes as Ramon and I clinked glasses. Then she looked up at him with a weary smile.

"You have to forgive my husband," Santos said. "He is my biggest fan."

"*La Soldadera* should be toasted every night!" Ramon said, and raised his glass. He took a sip, then set down his glass and looked at me. "So, *señor*, what is it you want to talk about? The money?"

I stared at Ramon with what I figured was a stunned expression on my face. The guy was way ahead of me and he knew it.

Santos shook her head wearily. "Ramon, please, not the money again."

"That's why he's here, isn't it?" Ramon said, locking eyes with me.

I put up my hands in what I imagined looked like surrender. "Look, I don't know anything about the money, okay?"

"Then why are you here? You think we know about it? You think I'd be a bartender if we knew about the money?"

Santos sighed. "Leave him alone, Ramon," she said. She turned to me. "Why did you want to talk to me?"

I pulled out the snapshot of Santos and Archie standing by the LeBaron in front of La Bahia and handed it to her. She smiled warmly at the sight of it.

"Where did you get this?" she said, her eyes on the

photo.

"His wife."

She looked up at me. "Daphne?"

I nodded.

"How is she?"

"As well as can be expected."

Santos gave a knowing smile. "Women like Daphne are always as well as can be expected."

Ramon snatched the photo away from her. He looked at it and scowled. "He owed you."

Santos rolled her eyes. "Oh Ramon, please, we've been over that a hundred times." She looked up at me. "Is this what you wanted to talk about? A snapshot?" she said, nodding at the photo.

"I like woodies. I saw the car out front. It's the same one, right?"

"*Si*, it is the same one. Archie liked woodies too. He only had one, but it was very rare."

"I'd love to see it."

"You should go to Woody Wonders. Maybe they'll show it to you."

"Woody Wonders?"

"The dealer in Alameda Point where Archie stored his car. Archie wanted me to store my car there too, but I like to keep it here at the club."

"We should sell his car," Ramon said. "He owes us that much."

"I think it was all talk," Santos said.

"The money?"

Santos nodded. "Archie wanted everybody to think he was a bigshot, you know what I mean? He wanted everybody to think that he was some kind of master thief who got away with a big score."

"So that's it, it was just talk?"

Santos shrugged. "Who knows? Only Archie knows and he's dead. Now he never has to prove the money's real and everybody can keep on believing that it's out there somewhere."

"It is out there," Ramon said. "We just have to find it."

"And what if what we find is nothing?"

"Then at least we'll know."

"He got away with the myth," Santos said. "That was what mattered to Archie. He wanted to be bigger than life, and I think he knew that even if he died, the myth of the master thief would outlive him."

"What about what he owed you?" Ramon said,

"What did he owe me? We were friends, we liked cars, so what?"

"He promised he would take care of you."

Santos paused, then looked at her husband, her eyes filled with love and sorrow. "I thought *you* promised to take care of me, Ramon."

Ramon met her gaze, then looked away. I knew this would go on for as long as they were together.

Santos looked up at me. "You wrote Archie's obituary, no?"

I nodded.

"But you can't let go of him, can you?" Santos said. "You're like everybody else, eh?"

I shook my head. "It's not him I can't let go of," I said.

She flashed that knowing smile again. "Of course. The grieving widow."

"Thanks for your time," I said. I stood and headed for the door. It was long past my bedtime and Daphne Swan was nowhere to be found.

Chapter 22

Traffic was light as I headed north on Interstate 880 toward the Bay Bridge, which gave me plenty of time to wonder why Daphne hadn't checked in at the Fairmont or returned any of my calls. Maybe something had gone wrong with the move and she was too busy to get back to me. Or maybe I just didn't want to face the fact that she was gone. Because if she was gone, what would I do without her? I wasn't ready to face that either, and so I decided that something had gone wrong and she needed my help. Just like she needed my help the night she gunned down Roy and Donny.

So instead of heading home to the Mission when I got to the city, I took the exit off 101 south to the Golden Gate Bridge and headed north to Marin. I knew the way, even in the dark. But as I followed the winding road into the hills, the night seemed even darker than usual, as if something was hiding there, something I should have known, but didn't.

I flashed on Mick and Janis as I passed the house that was still under construction, and now seemed like a house that would never be finished but would always be haunted by the ghosts who lived there. I saw no one out of the corner of my eye, but that didn't mean nobody was home.

The lights were off when I pulled up in front of Daphne's house, and the dark seemed to lay on the place like a shroud. But as I swung into the driveway and the headlights swept the house, I noticed that the front door was open. Maybe the movers forgot to close the door after they finished packing up, I thought. Or maybe Daphne left it open because she just didn't care. Whatever it was, it wasn't right. I rummaged for the flashlight I kept in the glove because when you drove an old car you never knew what could go wrong. Then I killed the engine and the lights and got out of the car.

I followed the flashlight's beam into the house. The living room was empty, and the stacks of boxes and artworks that had lined the walls were gone. The dining room was empty as well, and I was starting to get the feeling that probably the movers had left the door open by mistake. I felt like an intruder as I moved through the house, the flashlight's beam bouncing off the walls of empty rooms. Get out, I told myself. There's nothing to see here. Go home. You don't belong here. My thoughts were voices in my head as I scanned the rooms. But I didn't listen to them. I just kept following the flashlight's beam as it pulled me deeper into the house.

Then I went into Archie and Daphne's bedroom. The bed and the rest of the furniture were gone.

But the room wasn't empty.

Daphne was there.

She lay on her back on the floor in a pool of blood that shimmered in the flashlight's beam. Her eyes were open and I felt as if she was looking up at me from beyond the grave. I stared at her as the horror of what I was seeing nearly suffocated me. My legs felt rubbery and I grabbed the door to stop myself from collapsing on the floor beside her. I turned off the flashlight but even in the dark I could still see her. Daphne was dead and I

213

couldn't understand why she was dead or why she had suddenly disappeared from my life.

I ran out of the bedroom, stumbling in the dark, and slumped on the floor in the empty living room. I rocked back and forth like a child as a howl erupted from somewhere inside me. Why was she dead? Who killed her? What was she doing here after the movers had come and gone? Did she come back to make sure nothing was left behind? Was that when she was killed?

Questions ricocheted through my mind, but the answers were nowhere in sight. What should I do now, I wondered. Call the police? They would want to know what I was doing there in the middle of night. What about 911? I could make an anonymous call and hang up. But my cell number would show up. They would know it was me. I had no idea what to do. So I sat in the dark with Daphne, the two of us alone in the house together for one last time.

Then I thought of Daphne's cellphone, and realized that it had a record of all our calls, starting with the day I called to interview her for Archie's obituary. If the police got hold of the phone and saw the call history it could incriminate me. I realized that I had to find it. Which meant I had to search Daphne's body. I stood and went back into the bedroom.

I knelt beside her and bowed my head, as if I was praying for her. But the truth was I was praying for myself. I put the flashlight on the floor so that I didn't have to see Daphne's eyes watching me. I didn't want to touch her. I had wanted to touch her from the first moment I saw her, but this was different. Now I felt like a grave robber, searching for what I could steal to save myself. I reached out and ran my hand over her body, feeling for anything that felt like a phone.

I had never touched a dead body. I had written about the dead since the day I joined the *Bugle,* but I had never reached out and touched them. And now, as I ran my hand over her body, I felt as if I was caressing her one last time. My hands felt sticky and my clothes were smeared with blood. But the phone was nowhere to be found. I felt as if I was frisking the dead. Guilt and revulsion and nausea rose up inside me as the flashlight's beam shone on her face. What was the look in her eyes telling me? That she forgave my desecration? I dropped the flashlight and ran outside and threw up on the lawn.

Then I used the garden hose to rinse my hands and wash the blood and vomit off my face. I turned off the water and went back in the house to get the flashlight. I figured that whoever killed Daphne had also taken her phone. That at least would keep it out of the hands of the police. I picked up the flashlight and looked down at her one last time. I tried to think of something to say but my mouth was dry and I could feel the tears welling up in my eyes. Tears for us both, I thought, as I knelt beside her and kissed her cold, dead lips. Then I switched off the flashlight and walked out of the house.

I climbed back into the car. It was cold and I shivered as I sat behind the wheel. But I knew it was even colder in the house. I fumbled for the keys and was about to start the car when my cellphone rang. I pulled it out of my pocket and glanced at the screen.

And saw it was Daphne.

"Hi Max," a woman said. "I bet for a minute you thought it was her, huh?"

A chill ran down my spine. I tried to breathe but my lungs wouldn't cooperate.

"You see her?" the woman said. "You see what happened to her? She don't look so good now, does she?"

I looked down at my phone and launched the app that enabled me to record incoming calls. Nicole had installed it for me so I could record my interviews with friends and family of the deceased. But I never imagined that it would be used to record a call that, for a moment, seemed to come from beyond the grave.

"Who is this," I said, my voice a rasp in my throat.

The woman chuckled. "You'd love to know, wouldn't you?"

"Did you kill her?"

"She's dead, isn't she?"

"Why?"

"Why is she dead?"

"Yeah."

"Family business."

"I don't understand."

"You don't have to."

"So what do you want from me?"

"The money, silly. Archie's last big score."

"What makes you think I know anything about it?"

"You better know something about it, because if you don't, I'm turning Daphne's phone over to the cops. I'm sure they'd love to hear all about you and Daphne."

Then I heard what sounded like a baby crying. A man said, "Come on, Cathy, Roy Junior's waking up."

"Don't call him that," the woman called out. "His name's RJ."

"What the hell's going on?" I said. "Who are you?"

"Me? I'm the gal who's got you by the balls, Max. Either you find the money or the cops get the phone."

"I told you, I don't know about the money, okay?" I could feel myself breaking out in a cold, desperate sweat. How was I supposed to find Archie's treasure when I had no idea where it was or even if it existed?

"You've got three days. Oh, and if I were you I wouldn't stick around. I already called 911. I bet if you roll the window down you can hear the sirens."

The line went dead. But I didn't need to roll the window down. I could hear the sirens loud and clear, wailing through the hills, getting closer and closer.

I reversed out of the driveway and started down the dark and winding road that would take me back to the freeway. Then I saw the headlights of the black-and-whites lighting up the trees as the cops headed toward me, sirens wailing, roofs on fire. I pulled over and killed the lights, then ducked down until the cars flashed past me. I waited for the sirens to fade, then sat up again. I rolled the window down and the breeze made me feel as if the night had flowed into the car. Suddenly, I wanted the dark to absorb me, to hide me where no one would find me.

Forty minutes later, I drove into the overpriced parking garage three blocks from my building and pulled into my usual spot. I played back the call, then stepped out of the car and looked around for any signs of life. But I was the only sign of life, and at the moment I was barely hanging on. An empty Muni bus rumbled down Mission as I headed down the street to my building. The driver glanced at me, then kept rolling without missing a beat. I figured he'd seen plenty working graveyard, and a man walking down the street covered in blood was probably par for the course.

I took the stairs up to my floor. My apartment felt

colder than usual, and I wondered if death had followed me home from Daphne's house. I turned up the heat, then pulled off my clothes and stuffed them into a plastic garbage bag. Tomorrow I'd find a dumpster somewhere where I could dump them. Then I went into the bathroom and turned on the shower and waited for the stall to fill with steam clouds. Maybe the scalding hot water pouring down on me would wash away the feel of Daphne's cold, dead lips on mine.

But it was no use. I had felt her slipping away from me, but I never imagined it would be like this. That there would be no way back to her. That she was gone forever, dead as the subjects whose lives I memorialized for the *Bugle*. Who would write her obituary, I wondered. I wasn't sure I could do it. I wrote about strangers, never a woman who'd stolen my heart. What would I say about her? Would I describe how she looked the day I met her, fresh from the pool? The way she felt in my arms? What it was like to find her dead on the floor, her life spilled out around her?

The headline came to me as I closed my eyes and let the water wash over me: "Daphne Swan, Widow of Underworld Kingpin, Murdered in Marin at the Age of—" I stopped when I realized that I didn't know how old Daphne was. It was one of the many things I didn't know about her, and never had time to find out. But was it right to see her only as Archie's widow? Wasn't she more than that? She was to me.

I turned off the water and stepped out of the shower. I dried myself, then wiped the mist off the mirror and stared at the face that looked back at me. It was me, all right, but at the same time it wasn't me. Something had changed. Maybe it was the horror I saw in my eyes.

Suddenly, I never wanted to look at myself again. Because if I did, I would see it again. The snuff movie would start unspooling in my head and then Daphne would appear, sailing to eternity in a sea of blood.

But she wasn't alone. Roy and Donny were there too. Her house had once again become a crime scene, and I wondered what the new owners would make of it. I pulled on a pair of sweats and sank into a chair by the window. Then I picked up my cellphone and searched for news of Daphne's murder. But what was the point? I already knew the lede. I imagined Nicole hearing the call on her portable scanner and had to resist the urge to call her, seeing how it was past three in the morning.

My head was spinning with questions. Who was the mystery woman who called me? What did she mean when she said Daphne's murder was family business? Why did she think I knew where Archie buried his treasure? But she wasn't the only one. What about Benny and Ida Velasco, Lola and Ramon Santos, and Tiffany's Brazilian BF Ronaldo? They were all circling like sharks and I was the guy who'd forgotten how to swim.

Time was running out and I had no idea how to stop it. Three days, the woman said. What a joke. She may as well as given me a week or a month or a year. Turn the phone over to the cops now, I thought, and save us both the trouble. But then I saw myself trapped in a windowless interrogation room, waiting to be questioned about my relationship with the late Daphne Swan, and decided that three days were better than nothing.

But nothing was pretty much all I had to go on. All I did know was that when the woman called me I heard a baby crying in the background. She said his name was RJ. Or was it Roy Junior? What kind of clue was that?

219

The only one I had.

****

"A baby called RJ?" Nicole said as she sipped her latte.

We were sitting by the window at Grand Coffee, a coffee shop on Mission Street between 22nd and 23rd. The clock on the wall read ten, but to me it felt like the middle of the night.

"Yeah, or maybe Junior," I said. "Weird, huh?"

"Must be a nickname or something."

I shrugged. What did I know about kids. The dead were my beat.

"Boy or girl?"

"It was a baby, Nic. They all sound the same."

"Why does everybody think you know about Archie's score?"

"Beats me," I said with a shrug. "I guess they all think Daphne told me where he stashed it, but the funny thing is, I don't think she knew either."

"So what are you gonna do? She's got Daphne's phone. If the police get hold of it they'll bring you in for questioning."

"I've got three days to make sure that doesn't happen."

"That's not much time, Max. Anyway, you're not a detective."

I sipped my coffee. "I am now," I said. "Daphne's dead and somebody needs to pay."

"So what, you're judge, jury, and executioner now?"

I said nothing. I could feel Nicole watching me. I figured it wasn't a pretty sight. Kind of like when people drive slowly past a car crash hoping to catch a glimpse of the victims.

"You look terrible," she said.

I nodded. "Figured."

"You get any sleep?"

"Not yet."

"What were you doing there, anyway?"

"I hadn't heard from her."

"You mean she wasn't returning your calls," she said.

"Last time I saw her she told me she was gonna be at the Fairmont, but when I called they told me there was no one there by that name. So I decided to check up on her."

"In the middle of the night?"

"I thought maybe something was wrong."

"You couldn't let go, could you, Max?"

I looked up at Nicole, met the look in her cool blue eyes and turned away. I gulped my coffee, then grimaced as it burned my tongue.

Nicole offered a knowing smile as she shook her head. "You never learn, do you?"

I wasn't sure if she was talking about coffee or women, but the fact was I often got burned in both departments.

"So what about Archie's score?"

"I don't give a damn about the score, Nic. What I need to do is find whoever killed Daphne."

"You think she did it? The woman who called you?"

"She had her phone. She knew she was dead. If she didn't kill her, she knows who did."

"But how you gonna find her? You've got nothing to go on."

"Just RJ," I said.

"You call that a lead?"

221

I said nothing. Just looked around at the crowd in the coffee shop. Everybody looked pretty normal. I wondered if any of them had just spent the night with a corpse.

" You hear from Dan on what they found at the crime scene?"

Nicole sighed. "Not much. It's out of his jurisdiction, and anyway he's not too happy with me these days. He didn't appreciate me threatening to tell his wife about us. But you know what? He's pissed at me but he still wants to hook up." She gave a weary shrug. "Men." She said it like she'd had enough of us.

"So what are you gonna do—hook up with him anyway?"

"I don't know, maybe."

"So I guess I'm not the only one who can't let go."

"It's not so easy to let go, Max."

"Yeah, even when they're dead." I fell silent. I could hear the sounds of the living all around us. The hiss of the coffee machines, the clacking of computer keyboards, the chatter of conversations. And for some reason I thought about how silent the dead were.

"What's gonna happen to her?" I said.

"Daphne?"

I nodded.

"Her next of kin will claim the body."

"What if no one comes forward? Archie's dead and she didn't have any kids."

"She'll be cremated along with all the other unclaimed bodies."

"What happens to the ashes?"

"I'm not sure," Nicole said. "I guess they dispose of them somewhere." She looked up at me with a puzzled expression. "Why so many questions?"

"Just curious. Seems like a lonely way to go, nobody there to say a few words or whatever."

"She's dead, Max. I don't think she's gonna mind."

Nicole's cellphone pinged with a text. She glanced at the screen and frowned. "I gotta go," she said.

I nodded. "I'll leave the tip." I stood and reached into my pocket. A couple of singles tumbled out, along with some change and the Woody Wonders fridge magnet.

"Still carrying that around, huh?" Nicole said, nodding at the magnet. "Belongs on a refrigerator, you know."

"Yeah, I know. I guess I just can't let go of it."

"You mean you can't let go of her."

I shrugged. "Not yet anyway," I said, and slipped the magnet into my pocket.

Chapter 23

I didn't know how to look for a kid without coming off as a pedophile. But I did know the way to Alameda Point. So I signed out for lunch, drove across the Bay Bridge to Oakland, and then rode the Webster tube to Alameda Island. Alameda Point was on the west end of the island, and during World War II it was known as the Alameda Naval Air Station. It was one of the largest wartime naval stations in the world, with runways, seaplane ramps, docks for aircraft carriers, lighted seadromes, the works. When the Navy sailed away after the Cold War, they left behind hundreds of hangars, factories, and warehouses. Private enterprise moved in and now Alameda Point was filled with everything from condos, wineries and sports clubs to science labs, tech startups, bike shops, and the biggest monthly antiques fair in Northern California.

I wasn't looking for a condo or a wine tasting or a workout, and if it wasn't for the fact that Woody Wonders was also at Alameda Point I wouldn't have been there at all. I wasn't sure what I expected to find there beyond a warehouse full of old cars, and maybe that was enough for an afternoon. But Daphne's fridge magnet had brought me this far, and there had to be a reason why.

Maybe I should have been out looking for a baby instead of wasting my time looking at cars I could never afford. But I had no clue how to find baby RJ, and I figured the woman on the other end of the line knew that. So I went with the clue I had, and maybe somewhere down the line the two would meet up.

The first thing I saw as I pulled up in front of the dealership was the 1950s style neon sign that spelled out Woody Wonders. But it wasn't like they needed the signage. The vintage 1930s convertible and station wagon on display out front said it all. It was a sunny day, and the cars were sparkling like they were under a spotlight. I parked, then got out of the car and looked around. The warehouse doors were open and I could see more woodies inside. I decided to start with the cars on display. I didn't know much about woodies, but the cars on display appeared to be in mint condition, as if a time machine had somehow driven them decades into the future.

I was taking my time, no rush, when a man stepped out of the office and walked over to me. He was in his sixties, I guessed, around Archie's age when he died. He had wavy gray hair and a tan, wore a pink polo shirt, jeans, and aviator sunglasses, and looked like he was on vacation.

Then again, most car salesmen looked to me like they were on vacation, maybe because they just sat around most of the time waiting for a customer to walk in the door. I flashed on the car salesmen I used to see sitting in beach chairs outside the dealership wearing shades and short sleeves. But this guy wasn't selling transportation. He was selling desire, trailer queens that sold for top dollar and lived out their lives in secure, climate-controlled garages.

"Beauties, aren't they?" the guy on vacation said.

I nodded. You couldn't argue with the truth, so I didn't try.

He cocked his head at my car. "That's yours?"

"Yeah."

"Sixty-eight, three-ninety-six, right?" he said, rattling off the model year and the engine displacement.

I nodded.

"You looking to trade?"

I shook my head. "Nope, just looking."

"Devlin's my name," he said as he fished for a business card. "But most folks call me Dev."

"Max McQuinn."

"Anything in particular you're looking for, Max?" Devlin said as he handed me the card. "You must like woodies, or you wouldn't be here, right?"

"I was hoping to take a look at Archie Gibbs's woody."

Devlin stiffened at the mention of Archie's ride. "We don't show the car to the public. Archie was pretty strict on that point. Anyway, it's not for sale."

"Sorry to hear that, Dev. Lola Santos said I should come by and take a look at it."

He seemed to loosen up a bit at the mention of Santos's name.

"You know Lola?"

I nodded. "She's got a pretty sweet woody herself."

"Yeah, she does. I keep telling her she ought to let us take care of it, but I guess she wants to keep it close to home."

"Yeah, that's what she told me."

Devlin gave himself a moment to think it over, then smiled, and I figured I'd passed the test.

"Well, I guess we can make an exception, seeing as

how you're a friend of Lola's."

"Thanks, I appreciate it."

"Right this way," Devlin said, like he was showing me to my table, and we headed into the warehouse.

What I saw took my breath away. The warehouse was filled with classic woody station wagons, panel trucks, sedans, and convertibles. Wherever I looked, I saw beauty on wheels. The kinds of cars that crossed the block at high-priced auctions across the country and around the world. I noticed that some of the cars were hidden under car covers, while others were covered with dust. It was like a barn find, the dream every collector has of stumbling upon a barn somewhere filled with vintage cars, hidden for decades and waiting to be discovered. But this wasn't a barn. This was a warehouse, and it was filled not with one or two cars, but with dozens of cars.

Devlin must have read the look on my face as we walked through the warehouse because he turned to me and said, "Take your time, there's a lot to look at."

"These cars all for sale?"

"Not all of them. Some people just want a place to store their cars."

"Like Archie?"

Devlin nodded. "Archie was particular about where he stored his car."

"What's gonna happen to it now?"

Devlin shrugged. "That's up to his wife. I told her I was interested, but the last time I talked to her she told me she was thinking about putting it up for auction."

I stopped cold. Apparently, he hadn't heard the news. And for a moment it was as though Daphne was still alive.

I paused to let the moment linger, then said, "Daphne's dead. She was murdered last night."

Devlin's face went white with shock. He leaned against a sedan to steady himself, as if the news had knocked the wind out of him. He took a deep breath and opened his mouth like he wanted to say something.

"Murdered?" he managed to say. "Daphne?"

I nodded.

"I just spoke to her the other day…" He shook his head in dismay. "Jesus, I can't believe it. What the fuck happened?"

"I just saw the headline. That's all I know."

It was getting easier and easier to lie. I wondered if I'd learned that from Daphne.

"What about the cops?"

"I hear they're on the case."

Devlin looked up at me as a shadow of suspicion darkened his face. "How come you know so much about it?"

"I'm a reporter for the *Bay Area Bugle*. Saw it come across the wire."

"Is that why you're here? Because she's dead and you've got your eye on the car?"

I shook my head. "Like I said before, I just wanted to see it."

"Okay, well, it's over here," Devlin said in a defeated tone of voice. "I guess it don't matter much now who sees it."

He led me to a private showroom in the rear of the building and pulled out his keys. Then he opened the door and we went inside. He turned on the lights and the car appeared in front of me. In a warehouse full of beautiful cars, Archie's woody stood apart. The top was down and the chrome bumpers, fat white sidewalls, leather upholstery, and wood panels on the sides and the trunk lid sparkled under the lights.

"Looks like it just came off the assembly line, doesn't it?" Devlin said.

I nodded as I did a slow lap around the car. "Makes you want to climb in behind the wheel and go for a ride."

Devlin nodded. "I think everybody who sees the car feels that way." His face took on a puzzled expression. "Funny thing is, Archie never took it out for a ride. Just wanted to let it sit here." Devlin shrugged. It was one more thing that would never make sense.

"Nice color," I said, admiring the pale yellow shade that perfectly complemented the car's wood panels.

"It's called Yellow Lustre," Devlin said. "I think it was an original color, but I'm not sure about that. Archie would know, but of course…" his voice trailed off into silence.

"What's gonna happen to the car now?"

Devlin shrugged. "Hell if I know. Got to talk to my attorney about it. I don't know if Daphne or Archie had any next of kin. They never mentioned anybody…"

"That was his birthday," I said, nodding at the personalized plate that read '081552'. "August 15, 1952."

"Yeah, I know," Devlin said. "I asked Archie about it the first time I saw the car. But how did you know that?"

I shrugged. "I think I read it somewhere."

But why did I feel there was something else about the plate that sounded familiar? Something that had nothing to do with a gangster's birthday. Whatever it was, I couldn't place it at the moment. Maybe later it would come to me. Then again, maybe not.

Devlin's cellphone rang. He took the call, then said, "Hang on a minute." He looked over at me, "I guess we're about done here, right?"

"Thanks for your time," I said, and headed out of the warehouse.

"Let me know if you change your mind about your car," Devlin called out to me.

That'll be the day, I thought, as I stepped out into the sunshine and fished for my keys.

Traffic was heavy on the Bay Bridge, the way it was most afternoons, and by the time I got back to the city I'd blown deadlines that were due by the end of the day. Which meant I'd have to work late on the obits that had piled up in my absence. I'd done it before, even pulled all-nighters to make deadlines. I knew the dead wouldn't mind. That was why I liked working with them. The Ripper was another story.

"Where the fuck are you?" he shouted into the phone.

"I'm on the bridge."

"What the fuck you doing on the bridge? You forget you're on deadline?"

"No, haven't forgotten, just running late. I'll get it done."

"You want to keep working here, right, Max?"

"Yeah, sure I do."

"Prove it."

The phone went dead. I took a deep breath and let it out slow, then inched my way forward in a sea of bumper-to-bumper traffic. I was working two jobs—reporter and detective—but only one of them came with a paycheck. Trouble was, I was in too deep to stop playing detective, even though I had no idea what I was doing. But the story kept pushing me forward, and so did the woman who stole Daphne's cellphone, and maybe her life too.

I took the elevator three flights up and headed toward my apartment at the end of the hall. As I came up to the door I heard TV sounds, and wondered who'd decided to make themselves at home. I thought for a moment about calling Cornell for help, then turned the key and went inside. The TV was tuned to some daytime talk show and there was a guy sitting on the sofa with a gun in his hand. The same gun I took off him the last time he showed up. He had black curly hair, dark eyes, and a greasy, olive complexion. He wore cargo shorts and a gray fleece vest over a yellow soccer jersey, just like last time. His feet were propped up on the coffee table like he lived there.

"Hey, Max," Ronaldo said, "I was wondering when you were coming home."

"You should've told me you were coming. I could've baked a cake."

Ronaldo smiled. "We came by the other day but you weren't home."

"Yeah, so I heard."

"So what the hell, we figured we'd try again."

"We?"

Just then I heard the toilet flush and a moment later Tiffany appeared in the living room.

She smiled and said, "Hey Max, how you doing? Surprised to see me?"

"Yeah, I am."

"My lawyer got me a new trial, so I'm out on bail. Cool, huh?"

"Which you just violated," I said nodding at the gun. "You know that, don't you?"

Tiffany shrugged it off and joined Ronaldo on the sofa. "They're gonna have to find me first, 'cause we're gone as soon as we get the money."

"So where is it?" Ronaldo said.

I shook my head wearily. This déjà vu all over again stuff was getting old fast.

"Maybe you didn't hear me the last time," I said. "I don't know where it is. Never did, okay?"

Tiffany's face hardened. She grabbed the gun out of Ronaldo's hand and pointed it at me. I heard her click the safety off.

I sighed as I stared down the barrel of the gun. It didn't take much to kill somebody. All you had to do was pull the trigger. Even a bimbo like Tiffany could do it.

"You think that's gonna improve my memory, Tiffany?"

"It better, 'cause otherwise I'm gonna have to shoot you."

"And then what?" I said. "You think I'm gonna talk when I'm dead?"

"I don't know," Tiffany said, sounding confused. "So just tell us and I won't have to shoot you."

"How do I know you won't shoot me anyway?"

Tiffany grinned. "I guess you don't, huh?" She looked at Ronaldo. "We gonna shoot him anyway, babe?"

Ronaldo shrugged. "I guess we'll have to wait and see what happens."

I nodded. "Mind if I sit down? I'd rather not hit the floor when you shoot me."

"Sure, no problem, Max," Ronaldo said. "Make

yourself at home."

"Thanks," I said. I settled into one of the club chairs facing the sofa, then nodded at the gun. "Must be getting heavy, huh?"

"Yeah, it is kinda heavy," Tiffany said.

"You ever shoot anybody before?"

Tiffany shook her head. "Nope. Guess I'm a virgin, huh?" Then she giggled.

"So, one last time, Max," Ronaldo said. "Where the fuck is it?"

I shook my head. Enough was enough. "Pull the trigger, Tiffany. Maybe I'll remember when I'm dead."

Suddenly, there was a knock at the door. A hard, insistent knock, the kind that didn't bother with being polite.

"Police! Open up!" a man said.

Tiffany and Ronaldo exchanged confused glances.

"What the fuck?" Ronaldo said.

This wasn't part of the plan. His eyes darted around the room, as if he was looking for a place to hide.

"What do I do now?" Tiffany said. "Shoot him?"

Another knock on the door. Harder this time. I figured next they'd use the battering ram.

"Open up! Now!"

Then I remembered that in all the excitement of discovering Ronaldo on my sofa I'd forgotten to lock the door behind me when I walked into the apartment.

"Door's open!" I shouted.

Tiffany pulled the trigger. The round whistled past my head and tore into the wall, ripping out a chunk of plaster that spun around the room like shrapnel. Then the door flew open and Bellamy and Robinson burst into the room, guns drawn. Ronaldo's hands shot into the air but it was way too late. The cops opened fire. Tiffany and Ronaldo jerked like marionettes as the rounds slammed into them, then slumped against each other and bled out on my sofa.

My ears were ringing and the air smelled like gunsmoke. Bellamy and Robinson looked at me and shook their heads.

"Him again," Robinson said.

"No shit," Bellamy said. "What is it about you, McQuinn? Trouble your middle name or what?"

"I'm sure he's got a perfectly reasonable explanation for what just happened here," Robinson said.

"Can't wait to hear all about it," Bellamy said. He looked around the room and spotted the records that lined the wall. "Vinyl, huh?"

I said nothing.

"Old school, right?" Bellamy turned to his partner. "You like records, Robinson?"

Robinson scoffed. "Yeah, let's spin a few sides." She nodded at Tiffany and Ronaldo. "Maybe they'll wake up and dance."

Bellamy shook his head. "Always on the clock, aren't you, Robinson?"

"One of us has to be," Robinson said. She glanced at Tiffany and Ronaldo. "Call it in."

Then Cornell appeared in the doorway. His eyes widened as he stared at Ronaldo and Tiffany.

"What the fuck, Max?" he said.

Bellamy turned to him. "Who are you?"

"Cornell Washington. I'm the building manager."

I could see a crowd of curious neighbors gathering in the hallway behind Cornell, peering over each other's shoulders to get a glimpse of the dead.

"What happened?" Cornell said.

"Police action," Bellamy said. "I need you to clear the hallway, get everybody back inside their apartments. You think you can do that, Cornell?"

"Yeah, sure, no problem."

"Great," Bellamy said, and closed the door in Cornell's face.

I was still staring at Tiffany and Ronaldo when I heard Robinson call for backup. The dead were piling up around me faster than I could write their obituaries. And I wondered again, as I had since the day I took the job at the *Bugle*, who would write mine.

We waited with the dead until backup and the M.E. and forensics techs arrived, then Bellamy turned to me and said, "Let's go."

Chapter 24

I felt like a perp sitting behind a steel mesh cage in the back seat of a police car. The looks on people's faces as they glanced at me seemed to say that if I was in the back I had to be guilty of something. They were right. I was guilty of something. And I wondered how long it would take before Bellamy and Robinson figured it out.

Twenty minutes later I was sitting in a windowless interrogation room at the downtown cop shop listening to the intermittent buzz of the station's busted AC. Bellamy and Robinson were sitting across from me. I wondered if they were listening to it too.

"So, I guess you must be wondering why we showed up today—"

"I know why you showed up," I said, cutting him off. "Daphne Swan is dead."

Bellamy and Robinson traded glances, then looked at me.

"How do you know?" Bellamy said. "Were you there?"

Yeah, I was there, I thought. Saw her on her back in a pool of blood. Kissed her cold, dead lips.

"Nicole told me," I lied.

"Right, Nicole," Bellamy said. "I guess it pays to have a friend on the crime beat, huh?"

"So where were you last night between the hours of midnight and six am?" Robinson said.

"I was at a Latin club in Oakland called Bahia."

"All night?"

"I hung out for a while after hours."

"And then where'd you go?"

"I went home."

"Got anybody who can vouch for that?"

I thought of the Muni bus driver who saw me walking down Mission to my building covered in blood.

"No."

Bellamy and Robinson exchanged glances. Then Bellamy said, "You liked her a little, didn't you?"

I looked up at him.

"The deceased, I mean."

"Yeah, I guess so. Is that a crime?"

"Only if you killed her," Bellamy said. "Did she have any enemies?"

"Benny and Ida Velasco weren't too happy with her."

"Yeah, we saw the catfight. Quite a show. You think they killed her?"

I shrugged. "I don't know. Maybe you should ask them."

"We plan to," Bellamy said.

"You didn't kill her, did you, McQuinn?" Robinson said.

"Why would I kill her?"

"You tell me?"

"See, we really want to believe you, Max," Bellamy said. But here's the thing—you don't have an alibi. And without an alibi, you're a suspect. You know how it goes, right?"

"So you don't have an alibi, right?" Robinson said.

I shook my head. Bellamy and Robinson traded

glances again, then Robinson said, "Okay, let's switch it up and talk about what happened today. You want to tell us what that was all about?"

"Ever hear of Archie Gibbs?" I said.

Bellamy and Robinson traded glances.

"Sure, we have. Saw his obit in the *Bugle*. What's he got to do with the couple in your apartment?"

"Everything," I said.

"We're all ears," Robinson said.

"It's a long story," I said.

"We ain't goin' nowhere," Robinson said, "and neither are you."

I thought about where the story began, and flashed on the night at Daphne's house when I went from being an obituary writer to an accomplice. I could've started there, but why tell them the truth? I was working on my own version of the truth, and so I skipped to the part about the bodies that were, as the Ripper would put it, still warm. I explained that Tiffany used to be married to a guy named Vic Biderbecke, who ran a payday loan company called Paycheck Today.

Bellamy leaned in and stopped me there. "You mean like in the Paycheck Today job?"

I nodded.

"Go on."

I covered Tiffany and Ronaldo's phony kidnapping scam, and how Archie and his crew somehow got wind of an armored truck filled with Paycheck Today cash.

"They never found the truck, right?" Bellamy said.

"Right. The truck disappeared after the hijack and Archie was never charged."

"What about Biderbecke? Where does he fit into this?"

"Biderbecke needed to pay Tiffany's ransom. But he didn't have the money. So after the heist he cooked the books and filed a phony insurance claim to cover his losses. But it all fell apart and Vic went to prison for fraud."

"So what were Tiffany and Ronaldo doing in your apartment?"

"They thought I knew where the money was."

"The Paycheck Today job?" Robinson said.

"Do you?" Bellamy said.

I shook my head. "No, but everybody seems to think I do."

"Why's that?"

"Because I interviewed Daphne for Archie's obit, and everybody figured she told me where it was."

"But she didn't, is that it?"

"She didn't know either. That's what Benny and Ida Velasco were doing at her house when you showed up about the gun. They wanted to know about the money, and figured Daphne was holding out on them."

"So it's all about the money, is that it?"

It was all about the money right from the start, I thought, thinking about Roy and Donny and everybody that came after them. They were all chasing the money, and maybe somewhere Archie was laughing his ass off.

"Maybe not all of it."

"How's that?"

"Daphne's dead, and I don't know why," I said. I looked up at Bellamy and Robinson. "And neither do you."

I knew about the phone call, though. I could've played it for them. But I wasn't ready for them to know what I knew. Because if they heard the call then then they'd hear about all the times I called Daphne, and then they'd ask more questions I didn't want to answer. I didn't know what I meant to Daphne. Maybe nothing. But I knew what she meant to me, and I had to keep it to myself.

"So can I go now?" I said. "I'm on deadline."

Robinson locked eyes with me. "We're on deadline too, McQuinn. With murder. And ours is a hell of a lot more important than yours."

Bellamy gave himself a moment to think about it, then said, "Okay, you're free to go."

Robinson looked sharply at Bellamy. "You sure about that, Detective?"

Bellamy locked eyes with Robinson, then turned to me. "But I'd stick around if I were you. We'd hate to have to come find you if we had more questions."

I wasn't going anywhere. Hell, I couldn't even go home. My apartment had turned into a crime scene, which meant I had to wait for CSI to finish up and then for the clean-up crew to make it all go away. I thought of Ernie and Janelle, and where it all began. Like it never happened, Ernie promised me. And by the time he and Janelle were done, I believed him. But it was different this time. Maybe because it was my place, and I wasn't sure I could ever live there again. And even if I did, I'd still have to deal with Cornell and the bullet holes in the wall. Not to mention shopping for a new sofa I couldn't afford. And living with the ghosts of Tiffany and Ronaldo.

Nicole said I could crash at her place until the whole thing blew over, but I needed space, and crashing on her sofa wasn't going to cut it. So I decided to check into a motel until Bellamy gave me the all-clear. I needed to follow up on the phone call I received from the woman I assumed was RJ's mother, and there was only one person I knew who could help me with that. Whatever I was going to do now, I figured it would be somewhere outside the law, and the less Nicole knew about it the better for her sake.

****

I checked into Beck's Motor Lodge on Market Street. Got a room on the second floor with a view of the parking lot, and worked chasing deadlines until I was done. I finished up with an obit for a tennis pro who'd ruled the courts back in the day. He was buried with his favorite tennis racquet, which meant the headline practically wrote itself. I reviewed the drafts, then zipped the docs and sent them to the Ripper. He wouldn't see them until morning, but at least they'd be in his inbox, which would get him off my back, at least for the time being.

But the tennis pro buried with his racquet got me thinking of Archie and his woody. I wondered if he ever thought of anything as extravagant as being buried in his car. Would he have wanted the top up or down, I wondered, as they propped him up behind the wheel, shades on. Then I thought of the license plate on Archie's woody, and wondered why it was still on my mind. What was it about it that was still nagging me? There was only one way to find out. I logged in to the *Bugle's* intranet, then pulled up Nicole's story on the Paycheck Today heist.

I got as far as the first paragraph when I realized why the date had stuck with me. Archie hijacked the armored truck on August 15, 2016. August 15 also happened to be Archie's birthday. So, was he celebrating his birthday when he used the date on his personalized plate? Or was there more to it than that? I needed to see the car again. But how exactly was I going to do that? I logged off, grabbed my keys, and closed the door behind me.

I was heading to the stairs when a door popped open and Benny Velasco emerged from a room. He wore khaki shorts and a pink polo shirt, and was carrying a bucket. I figured he was on his way to the ice machine. We both stopped at the sight of each other.

"Well, look who's here," Benny said.

I smiled politely. "Hey Benny, where's Ida?"

Benny frowned. "Where she belongs. Besides which, it's none of your business."

I put up my hands. Benny must have been born spoiling for a fight, I thought. "Just asking, Benny."

Benny's face hardened. "Just asking, huh? What do you say I ask you something?"

"You mean like where's the money, right?" I said.

The bucket fell out of Benny's hands and he slammed me up against the wall. "Yeah, that's what I'm gonna ask you. So where the fuck is it?"

A redhead half Benny's age and wearing a slip poked her head out of the room, saw the bucket on the landing and frowned.

"Benny, what the fuck? You gonna get the ice or what?"

I glanced at the redhead, then shook off Benny. "Give my regards to Ida" I said, then headed out to the car.

Chapter 25

His name was Vincent Devereaux, and if he was still above ground he lived in a trailer park on the outskirts of the city. It was after midnight by the time I found the place, and the rundown, ramshackle trailers looked even shabbier than the last time I'd been there. How long ago was that? I couldn't remember. But the trailer park seemed like one of those places that everyone forgot about, a way of life left behind in the rush toward better things. Which of course was the way Vincent liked it. He wanted to be forgotten, anonymous, invisible. Right now, I'd settle for still breathing. I pulled up by the entrance and got out of the car, then walked through the rusted gate toward what I hoped was a trailer that Vincent still called home.

Most of the trailers looked abandoned, and I wondered if I was too late. I hadn't seen or heard from Vincent since he went off the grid, off the radar, and nearly off the planet. But then I heard the snarl of late seventies punk, and saw that the lights were on in a trailer at the far end of the park. I smiled. Mr. D was alive and well.

I stepped up to the trailer and knocked on the door. I heard the scratch of a needle scraping across a record and the music stopped. A moment later the door flew open and I found myself staring down the business end of a double-barrel shotgun. The man holding the gun like he was used to it was in his late fifties and out of shape, with a paunch and shoulder-length blond hair that was going dirty gray. He had a pockmarked face and a pale complexion, and looked like he hadn't shaved in a week. He wore a faded heavy metal T-shirt and torn jeans, and his arms were splashed with tattoos.

"Max?"

"Yeah, it's me, Vincent. You want to put the gun down?"

Vincent lowered the shotgun. "What the fuck you doin' out here? Come to see if I'm still alive?"

I smiled. "I need your help, Mr. D."

Vincent looked around the trailer park, but all anybody could see were rundown, rusty trailers draped in shadows. "You took a chance comin' out here, you know. Anybody follow you?"

"Not that I know of."

Vincent gave himself a minute to think it over, then put down the gun. "Then I guess you better come inside."

He held the door open and I stepped inside. The trailer was a jumble of vinyl records, turntables, papers, manuals, books, and magazines, and it bristled with computers, modems, routers, monitors, and electronic equipment. Cables snaked from one end of the trailer to the other. The sink was filled to overflowing with dirty dishes and glasses, and the walls were covered with tattered vintage posters for legendary rock bands.

Vincent loved records as much as I did, though his taste ran more to punk and metal than midcentury jazz. But nostalgia only went so far. Apart from the vinyl and the posters and the turntables, there was nothing retro about Vincent's technical chops. Which is why I was there. Back in the day, Vincent had been a software developer who liked fast cars. But after he got a series of speeding tickets that cost him thousands of dollars, he decided to strike back. He created an app that enabled users to delete their speeding tickets from the system. The city took a dim view of his innovations, and Vincent had been on the run ever since. But that was then. What about now? I was betting that time had not dulled his genius or lack of respect for authority, even though he looked like a man who was barely hanging on to what was left of him.

Vincent plopped into a desk chair and looked at me. "You want a beer?"

"I wouldn't mind," I said.

"Right behind you," Vincent said, pointing at a refrigerator.

I opened the refrigerator, took out two beers, and handed one to Vincent. He twisted off the tab, tipped the bottle my way and took a deep swig. Then he looked at me.

"You still writing obits for the *Bay Area Bugle*?

I nodded.

"How'd you know I'd still be here?"

I shrugged. "I didn't, just hoped you would be."

"So how can I help you, Max? I don't know much about dead people, other than that they're dead."

"You're the only person I know who can help me, Vincent."

Vincent helped himself to another swig of beer. "I'm listening."

I started with Daphne, where the blood first began to flow, and told him everything I hadn't told Bellamy and Robinson. The dead all made an appearance—Roy, Donny, Ernie, Janelle, Mick, Janis, Rikers, Tiffany,

Ronaldo—before exiting stage right into eternity. And as the body count kept growing, I could see Vincent watching me with a stunned look on his face. In the end I circled back to Daphne, and the call I received from her phone.

Vincent had remained silent while I braced him on the events that had led me to his door in the middle of the night. And now, as I fell silent, there was nothing to listen to except the sound of a midnight wind whipping through the park, rattling the trailers.

"Shit, that's one hell of a story, bud," Vincent said.

I nodded. "Yeah, it is, and the worst part is it's true."

"So this all started with you writing some gangster's obit?"

"Yeah, and then it snowballed from there."

"Never thought the dead could be so much trouble."

"They weren't, until I met Daphne."

Vincent gave a knowing smile. "Some women are just flat-out dangerous, Max."

"Yeah, especially when they have a gun in their hand."

"So where do I come in?"

"I need to find out who called me from Daphne's phone. I was hoping maybe you could trace it."

"Yeah, maybe I can. But then what?"

"She's gonna turn the phone over to the cops if I don't dig up Archie's buried treasure."

"So where's the buried treasure?"

I scoffed. "Who knows, Vincent. I sure don't."

"So you need to get the phone before she gives it to the cops."

I nodded. "But that's not all."

Vincent looked up at me and waited for the rest of

it.

"She may have killed Daphne."

Vincent took a moment to let it sink in, then said, "I'll see what I can do."

I played records, killing time at 33 1/3 rpm while Vincent used his skills to trace the call from Daphne's cellphone. The sixties and seventies roared out of the speakers as I spun tracks from bands whose names were often the best thing about them. Vincent had all their records, just as I had all mine. And it struck me that we were both lost in the past when it came to music, but it was a past composed of different worlds.

Then Vincent stepped to the amplifier and turned down the volume. I looked up at him.

"You got something?"

Vincent nodded. "Pull up a chair."

We sat down in front of a large monitor on his desk. A map was on the screen.

"I traced the call," Vincent said. "This is where it came from." He pointed to a dot on the map. "Richmond."

"You got an address by any chance?" I said,

Vincent grinned, then scrolled down to reveal the address of a 7-Eleven store.

"So she made the call from a 7-Eleven store?"

Vincent nodded. "Or maybe the parking lot. But that's where it came from."

I was impressed. Vincent was an artist, I thought, and code was his canvas. I hoped the city never caught up with him.

"Good job, Mr. D," I said.

Vincent leaned back and crackled his knuckles. "All in a night's work," he said.

Robert Baty

"I'd ask you how you did it, but I wouldn't understand anyway," I said.

Vincent grinned. "No, you wouldn't. But you still got to find her."

"She had a baby with her, said his name was RJ. Maybe she takes him with her when she goes to 7-Eleven?"

Vincent nodded. "So what are you gonna do when you find her?"

"Get Daphne's phone before the cops do."

Vincent leaned back and took a swig of beer. "Sounds like a plan. So, anything else I can help you with?"

"There is one more thing, now that you mention it."

****

The lights were off at Woody Wonders, and the woodies that had been on display out front were gone. I figured they were safely tucked away inside the warehouse. But there was only one car I was interested in.

"I can't believe you talked me into this," Vincent said as we pulled up in front of the dealership.

"It'll be fun, Vincent. Kind of like the old days."

Vincent scoffed. "Nothin's like the old days, Max."

I killed the engine and turned off the lights, then climbed out of the car. Vincent reached for his cellphone and began working on hacking into the dealership's security system. I opened the trunk and pulled out the flashlight, then waited while Vincent worked his magic. The parking lot was deserted and there was no one around, but it still made me nervous to be standing by the only car in the lot. What if a cop working graveyard drove by and saw us? How would I explain what we were doing there? I leaned into the car and looked at Vincent.

"How it's going?"

"It's going."

"I don't like standing out here."

"Then wait in the car."

"What if somebody sees us?"

Vincent looked up from his phone. "You want to abort, Max?"

I paused, then shook my head. "Just don't want to get caught."

"Nobody's gonna get caught, okay? So just chill. I'm almost there."

I nodded and got back in the car. I took a deep breath, then began drumming my fingers on the steering wheel. Vincent looked over at me.

"You mind?" he said.

"Sorry."

I glanced at my watch. It was just after last call. I pictured the drunks stumbling out of Alameda bars and trying to remember where they parked their cars. Then I worried they might show up, having lost their way on the drive home. What was I doing out here in the middle of the night? What had my life become?

"Okay, let's do it," Vincent said, interrupting my thoughts.

We traded glances, then climbed out of the car and walked around the warehouse until we found a back door. I looked around while Vincent picked the lock, then we stepped inside and closed the door behind us. I switched on the flashlight and the beam danced across a sea of cars.

"Wow," Vincent said, his voice filled with awe. "This is really cool. Maybe I'll hotwire one of these babies and drive it home."

I wasn't sure if Vincent was kidding or not, and that was the part that scared me.

"Let's go," I said. "The car's back here."

We followed the flashlight's beam to the showroom with Archie's woody. Vincent picked the lock and we stepped inside.

"So this was Archie's ride, huh?" Vincent said.

I nodded.

"So what are we looking for, Max?"

"I'm not sure. I guess I'll know when I find it."

"Sooner the better would be good," Vincent said.

"Got it," I said.

I opened the door on the driver's side and got in the car. It must have been fun to drive a car like this, I thought, as I sat behind the wheel. I pictured Archie and Daphne out for a ride with the top down, and wondered if it ever happened. I checked the glove compartment, but all I found were the manuals that came with the car back in the day.

"Anything?"

I shook my head. I looked under the seats, then climbed out of the car.

"What about the trunk?"

"Let's take a look."

I walked around the car and pulled on the handle to open the trunk.

"It's locked," I said. "We need the keys to open it."

"So where are the keys?"

I shrugged. "No idea."

"Let me see if I can open it," Vincent said.

"Be my guest."

Vincent fiddled with the lock while I worried about

getting caught.

"Got it," he said, after what seemed like an eternity.

I smiled. "You ever consider a career in breaking and entering, Vincent?"

He grinned as I opened the trunk. I shone the flashlight on the contents, and what I saw took my breath away.

The trunk was filled with cash bags, the kind used by armored car companies. Vincent and I traded stunned glances.

"Holy shit!" Vincent said.

I stared at the cash bags, and flashed on how much blood had been spilled in search of them.

"I can't believe we found it," I said. I looked at Vincent. "It was there all the time."

"He buried his treasure in the trunk," Vincent said. "And nobody ever thought to look there. Crazy, huh?"

"Yeah, crazy," I said.

"How much you figure is here?"

"I don't know. Let's find out." I reached for a bag and opened it, then pulled out a stack of cash wrapped in a currency band. I shone the flashlight on the cash and gasped.

"Play money!" I said, looking at the bills. "It's play money, Vincent!"

Vincent and I traded shocked glances, then reached into the trunk and pulled out more stacks of cash, all of which were play money.

Vincent looked at me with a stunned expression. "Play money? Fucking play money? What the fuck, Max?"

"I don't get it," I said. "Why would he do that?"

"You're asking me?"

That was when we heard the sirens.

"Cops? Who would've called it in?"

"Nobody," Vincent said. "It must've triggered a silent alarm when I disabled the security system. We need to get out of here now."

I reached for my cellphone and snapped some pics of the cash, just for the hell of it. Then we stuffed the fake stacks back in the bags. I was about to close the trunk when I heard a familiar voice.

"About time you found it," Benny Velasco said. "What the fuck took you so long?"

I looked up and saw Velasco standing by the door with a gun in one hand and a flashlight in the other. I realized he must have been following me ever since I left the motel.

"It's not what you think it is, Benny."

"I'll be the judge of that. Step away from the car."

The sirens got louder.

"What's going on, Max? Who is this guy?"

"I'll tell you later. Let's get out of here." I looked at Velasco. "It's all yours, Benny."

"You bet your ass it is," Velasco said.

Vincent and I made our way through the warehouse toward the back door. We slipped out of the warehouse, then moved away from the building. I pointed to the condo complex that was under construction next to the warehouse. Vincent nodded and we made our way into the structure. We hid in the shadows behind a partially built wall and looked out at the entrance to the dealership.

"I don't think we can make it to the car before the cops show up," I said.

Vincent nodded. "Let's just hang here until the

show's over."

Just then the front door of the dealership crashed open and Velasco emerged with cash bags in both hands. As if on cue, police cars appeared, red and blue lights flashing. Velasco stopped cold, apparently stunned by the sight of them. Doors flew open and uniforms jumped out of their cars. Trained their guns on Velasco.

"Drop the bags!" a uniform commanded.

Velasco did as he was told and dropped the bags. Stacks of play money tumbled out onto the pavement. He stared at the play money, his face a mask of confusion and disbelief.

"Hands in the air!" the uniform commanded.

Velasco raised his hands. A uniform came up to him and cuffed him. He was still looking over his shoulder at the play money blowing across the lot as the uniforms led him to a black-and-white and shoved him into the back seat.

Vincent and I waited until the cops drove away, then emerged from the construction site and walked back to the car.

"Who was that guy?" Vincent said as we drove away.

"Just about the last one left alive who was chasing the money."

Vincent shook his head as he looked out the window. "Play money?" He turned and looked at me. "I mean, how in hell do you rob an armored truck full of play money?"

I glanced at him. "Beats me. But the only guy who knows ain't talking."

Chapter 26

I dropped Vincent off at his place, then headed back to the motel and crashed out cold until my cellphone woke me a little after ten.

"You okay?" Nicole said. "I haven't heard from you."

"Yeah, I'm okay." I rubbed the sleep out of my eyes. "We found it, Nic."

"Found what? What are you talking about?"

"Archie's big score."

"You found it?" Nicole said, her voice filled with excitement.

"Meet me at Grand Coffee and I'll tell you all about it."

Twenty minutes later Nicole and I huddled by the window with our coffee.

Nicole sipped her latte, then looked up at me. "It doesn't make sense, Max. Why would Archie hijack a truck filled with play money, and then hide it in the trunk of his woody?"

"No, it wouldn't have made sense to Archie. But maybe it did make sense to Vic Biderbecke."

"The Paycheck Today guy?"

I nodded. "What if Archie was set up and didn't know it until it was too late?"

"How do you mean?"

"Vic was hard up for cash, but he needed money to

254

ransom Tiffany, who was supposedly being held captive in Rio. So he put out the word that he was making a big deposit via armored truck. Then he filled the cash bags with play money. Archie took the bait and hijacked the truck and Vic filed an insurance claim for the loss. But it all fell apart for him when the insurance investigators discovered he'd cooked the books. Fell apart for Tiffany too, when the cops discovered the kidnapping was a scam."

"What about Archie? He didn't know he'd hijacked a truck full of play money?"

"Not until it was too late. And when he discovered the truth, he was too embarrassed to admit it. How could a master thief admit he'd just stolen play money? It would have humiliated him."

"So he hid the money in the car."

"Right. And then he let the heist become a legend. Which was way more important than the truth."

"But at some point they would have found the play money when the car was auctioned or something," she said.

"Didn't matter because by then Archie was dead. He'd managed to keep the myth as long as he was alive. If it died after that, so what?"

Nicole's face took on a somber expression. "All those people who died...they died for nothing, Max. For play money."

I nodded, and we both fell silent, as if out of respect for the dead. Then I looked up at Nicole.

"I want to claim her body, Nic..."

Nicole looked up at me. "Daphne?"

I nodded. "I don't know if anybody's come forward. Can you help me with that?"

"Sure, no problem. What do you want to do?"

I paused. What I wanted to do was the last thing I imagined I would ever have to do for Daphne. "I want to have her cremated and then scatter her ashes. Will you come with me?"

Nicole gave a sad and tender smile. She reached across the table and took my hand. "Sure."

Then both our cellphones pinged with texts, and it was time to go back to work.

I spent the rest of the day doing my job, which meant filling the Ripper's inbox with obits copy. Hour after hour, as traffic hummed on Market Street and the sounds of other lives seeped through the room's thin walls, the dead stopped by my desk for their final sendoff.

Late in the day, as shadows lengthened across the motel parking lot, I took a break and pulled up directions to the 7-Eleven store in Richmond from where the call was made. My plan was to drive out there and hang out in the hopes of seeing a woman with a baby called RJ or Roy Junior. But the more I thought about it, the more implausible it became. Was I going to stake out the store every night? How would I know it was her? What if she never showed up? And even if I did find her, then what? She wanted to trade Archie's score for Daphne's phone. But I doubted that a cash bag full of play money would have satisfied her.

But it was more than that. I realized I was just trying to save my own skin, when what I should have been doing was saving my soul. If she killed Daphne, then she should be prosecuted for her crime. I owed Daphne that much. Which meant that the police needed to know what I knew. They needed to hear the call. I played it back one more time, and when I heard the man refer to "Roy

Junior," something clicked and I almost fell out of my chair. If there was a Roy Junior, that meant there had to be a Roy Senior. And then I thought of Roy and Donny, and realized that the woman had to be Roy's widow. Daphne had killed her husband and the father of her child, and she had apparently returned the favor. I knew too much to keep it to myself any longer. I reached for my cell and made the call.

****

"So you *were* there?" Bellamy said after listening to the call the woman named Cathy made from Daphne's phone.

We were sitting in an interrogation room. It looked just like the last one, but at least this time the AC was working.

"Yeah, I was there."

"Why did you go up there?" Robinson said.

"I was worried. I hadn't heard from her, she hadn't returned my calls. I thought maybe something had happened to her. And then I found out that something did happen to her."

"Why didn't you report it then?"

"I guess I didn't want to have to explain what I was doing there. And the woman on the phone told me she'd called 911. Then I heard the sirens and I took off."

"So you ran," Bellamy said. "I thought you cared about her, McQuinn. Isn't that what you told us the last time?"

I paused. "Last time I was here you asked me if I liked her a little. The truth is I liked her a lot, Detective. Maybe I shouldn't have, but I did."

"Is that why you're coming forward now?" Bellamy said.

"I think the woman who called me from Daphne's phone murdered her, and I don't think she should get away with it."

"You know we could charge you with obstruction of justice," Robinson said. "And that's just for starters."

That's not the only thing you could charge me with, I thought. But I wasn't ready for the whole truth. Just enough truth to take down whoever killed Daphne.

"Yeah, I know. But I guess I couldn't live with her killing Daphne and getting away with it. So I had to come forward, no matter what it cost me."

"You fell in love with her," Robinson said. "That's what it's gonna cost you."

They let me go after that. I didn't know whether they'd charge me or not, and I figured they didn't know either, or they wouldn't have let me go. But I knew they'd decide soon enough, and until then I was in a kind of no man's land, somewhere between a free man and a felon.

And yet for some weird reason I was okay with it. I'd never fallen hard the way I fell for Daphne, and it felt good even as it tore me up. Maybe that was love the hard way. But now that she was dead I didn't want to let go of her. I wanted her to be mine now, all the way to the end. And if no one else claimed her body, she would be. The last thing I wanted was for the city to cremate her and dump her ashes in some potter's field that was filled with the remains of unknown or unclaimed people.

Chapter 27

The news came across Nicole's scanner not long after my interview with Bellamy and Robinson. An unidentified male and female living in an apartment complex in Richmond had been arrested without incident on suspicion of murder. An infant found on the premises had been turned over to child protective services. There was no word yet on whether the woman, or the woman and her male companion, had confessed to the murder of Daphne Swan.

Meanwhile, no one came forward to claim Daphne, which made me feel lonely for her. I didn't want anyone else claiming her, and yet I couldn't help wondering if I was the only person alive who cared for her. Nicole informed me that the M.E. had completed his examination and Daphne's body was available for release. We made arrangements with a place out on Geary called Better Cremation Care and they sent a hearse to pick her up. I tried to follow the hearse, but lost sight of it in traffic. I guess I wanted Daphne to know that she wasn't alone, that I was right behind her. But it didn't work out that way.

The waiting room at the crematorium had a window with a view of the cremation chamber. It featured a conveyor belt and what looked like an oven large enough to incinerate a human being. But they didn't call it an oven. They called it a cremator. Nicole and I stood by the window and watched as Daphne's casket was placed on the conveyor belt and then rolled toward the cremator. Then the cremator's door opened and I could see a sudden flash of flames. They slid Daphne into the cremator, then the door closed, and she was gone.

Nicole asked me if I wanted to stay overnight with her rather than at the motel, but I told her I needed to be alone. I wanted my room at Beck's Motor Lodge, a place without a past, present, or future. I needed to be nowhere, at least for one night. I didn't get much sleep, but when I did I dreamed that Daphne and I were taking a drive in Archie's woody. The sun was out and the top was down, and Daphne wore shades that made her look like a movie star. I remember her asking me where we were going, and I told her we were lost. She smiled like she knew all along we were lost. Then I woke to the sound of trash trucks picking up garbage on Market Street.

Later that morning, Nicole and I went back to the crematorium and they handed me an urn filled with what they called Daphne's cremains. But to me it was filled with her. We drove to out to Clipper Yacht Harbor in Sausalito, then sat in the car and looked out at a boat. It was called the Blue Runner and according to the website it was certified by the U.S. Coast Guard.

"Nice day, huh?" Nicole said, looking out at the water shimmering in the sun.

I nodded. The sunlight seemed so alive, so at odds with being dead.

"You ready for this?" she said.

"I've never done this before, Nic."

She was sitting next to me and the urn I'd bought at the crematorium's retail shop was in her hands. Which was another way of saying that Daphne, or whatever she'd become, was in her hands.

"Which part? Being in love or saying goodbye?"

I looked at her and offered a rueful smile. "Both, I guess."

"C'mon, let's do it then."

We climbed out of the car and headed down the ramp to the boat.

"Welcome aboard," a man said as we boarded the ship. "I'm Captain Cook."

Cook was in his forties, I figured, tanned and wearing a yacht captain's cap, and he looked as if he'd spent the last twenty years at the helm. I thought of the ferryman I'd read about years ago in my college Greek mythology class who carried the souls of the deceased across the river that divided the living from the dead.

"Thanks," I said.

"Just a party of two?" Cook said.

"Plus the deceased," I replied.

"Did you bring rose petals?"

"Rose petals?" I said.

"We usually like to make three passes," Cook explained. "The first pass gives you an opportunity to toss rose petals into the water. On the second pass, we circle back and sail through the petals, and then on the third pass you scatter the ashes. The families seem to like that approach."

"It's just us," I said glancing at Nicole, "so we can just skip to the part where we scatter the ashes."

"No problem," Cook said. "Take your seats and we'll be on our way." He turned and headed toward the bridge.

Nicole and I sat on a bench on the rear deck. Moments later I heard the ship's engines rumble to life and we headed out to sea.

We sailed out past the Golden Gate to where the Marin Headlands provided shelter from the wind. A deckhand informed us that we had a choice of locations to scatter the ashes. We could choose Kirby Cove, a quiet spot by the Golden Gate, the calm waters off Angel Island, or in front of the San Francisco skyline.

I turned to Nicole. "I think she'd like the skyline."

Nicole nodded. I felt the boat slow as Cook positioned it to face the skyline. I paused for a moment to reflect on how we all went up in smoke, then I stood and held the urn out to sea. I watched as Daphne's ashes swirled into the breeze blowing toward the city.

I turned to Nicole and smiled.

"What's so funny?"

"Daphne told me she always wanted to live in the city."

"I guess she finally got her chance."

As we headed back to port, I pictured Daphne somewhere in the San Francisco wind that blew through city streets, moving, never resting, always there.

A word about the author…

Robert Baty is based in the Bay Area, and writes crime fiction because when you live in a city as dangerous as Oakland, it seems the only way to tell the truth. His publishing credits include "The Blonde in the Lotus Elite" and "The Girl in the MGA," two mysteries set in the world of classic cars; "Murder Goes on Tour," a standalone mystery; and "The Haunting of Tana Grant," a ghost story set in San Francisco. When he's not following his characters down the mean streets of his imagination, Bob is piloting his vintage Alfa Romeo through the blind curves that lie just ahead.

https://www.amazon.com/author/robertbatybooks

Milton Keynes UK
Ingram Content Group UK Ltd.
UKHW031617231124
451036UK00001B/7

9 781509 257393